Close the window

Stefan

(dyslexia-friendly   edition)

Published by Crossbridge Books
Worcester   WR6 6PL
www.crossbridgeeducational.com

ISBN   978 1 913946 21 0

British Library Cataloguing in Publication Data
A catalogue record for this book is available from the British
Library

CROSSBRIDGE
BOOKS

Close the window

Stefan

(dyslexia-friendly   edition)

R M MACE

For Dad

Part One
Chapter One

The sound of a siren screamed in Stefan's head. The wail seemed to flow through his veins and explode from the ends of his fingers and toes. His bed was shaking as if in the grip of a terrible earthquake.
'Wake up,' his mother was saying, 'and don't forget your pillow'.
Stefan forced himself awake. He pulled off his nightshirt, groped in the darkness for his shorts and shirt that were laid out in readiness, and slipped easily into them. It was a well-rehearsed ritual. He silently felt for his socks and shoes, snatched up his pillow and ran.
Stefan hurried down the stairs in the dark, clutching his pillow and picturing in his mind's eye every turn of the stairs. The stairwell was always kept clear. He could hear his father's urgent whispers tinged with anxiety. His mother was heavily pregnant and Stefan could hear her laboured breathing as she hurried down the stairs.

The late-summer air was warm outside. The feeling of heat was accentuated by the dark orange glow that lit up the night sky over Mannheim. There was no wind, but the air seemed to reverberate between the buildings. The ground was rocked by the dull thud of explosions that were, for the moment, in the distance. The bombing had begun in May and had continued through the summer – it now seemed to be part of their daily routine.

As Stefan crossed the street outside their apartment, at full speed alongside his father, he heard a muffled cry and the sound of his mother's body crumpling to the ground as she tripped and fell. His father ran back, helped her to her feet, and half carried her to the shelter.

The shelter was in the cellar of an old brewery. The ceilings were low, but vaulted rather like a crypt in a cathedral. It was all made from local sandstone that was rough and warm to the touch. Stefan felt his way down the steps in the dark and headed towards the dim glow of candles. A dozen people were already there, huddled into corners. The candles were on the floor and flickered eerily each time the ground nearby was pounded by a bomb, casting looming shadows on the walls.

Stefan's father helped his mother onto a small cushion that he had remembered to bring. For his mother, who was expecting a baby, sitting on that hard stone floor would have been very uncomfortable. Nobody spoke – they were praying. Most of the people in that cellar were Catholics. The night raids would last for long hours – aircraft can't stand still. They came and dropped some of their payload, then would turn around over the forest and come again.

Gradually, in the dim light, Stefan could see the dust from the floor begin to rise as the vibrations from the explosions intensified.
'Pick up your pillow Stefan,' said his father as he buried his own face into his feather pillow. Stefan pushed his face into his pillow, making sure that it was stretched taut so that he could still breathe. In the early days of the air raids, people had suffocated from the dust in their shelters – now people took pillows with them to filter out the dust.

Eventually the sound of explosions stopped. In the cellar people sat still, listening; knowing they would be needed to help with the fires but reluctant to have to face the horrors once again. Stefan's father had been put in charge of organising supplies for the local community and so was one of the first to move.
'Come Stefan, we must take your mother home to rest and then see what must be done. There will be fires to put out.' His father spoke in a simple matter-of-fact way; there were no complaints or fears, just a determination to get on with living.

Outside, the air seemed to be just as thick with dust, but there was the added smell of smoke and burning rubble. The family hurried back to the building where they had an apartment on the first floor. The house had not been damaged in the raid. Once inside, Stefan's mother went straight to bed, and his father went out to see if help was needed.

'Stay with your mother until I come back,' said his father before disappearing back down stairs.

Stefan went to the window, pulled up the wooden shutters and looked out into the night sky. Over Mannheim the sky was almost red. Nearby, fires were still raging. Stefan hadn't seen his friend Julius in the shelter.

'He probably just went down into the house cellar,' Stefan thought to himself, 'I expect his mother and sister couldn't get out fast enough'.

Julius lived in the next apartment on the same floor. They were good friends. Julius was just one month older than Stefan and had a younger sister Anneliese. Stefan's thoughts were interrupted by the sound of his mother groaning. He hoped the fall hadn't hurt her too much.

'Stefan! Come quickly,' he heard his father's urgent call 'your aunt Liesle's house is burning.'

Stefan followed his father towards the burning building where a crowd had already gathered to help. They were passing buckets to douse the flames. As they approached, Stefan was handed a bucket and told there was no more water.

'Go over there to fill the bucket,' said his father, pointing to where the others were filling their buckets.

It was a pit for sewage. Stefan obediently filled his bucket and carried it towards the burning building. It was very heavy and the smell was awful. The bucket was emptied and handed back to him. Stefan refilled the bucket and staggered back with it. It was too heavy for him to carry all the way. His father picked up the bucket 'I'll take it from here, you've done enough. We'll save the house, go back to look after your mother,' he said in a voice that was slow with weariness.

As Stefan mounted the stairs to the first floor of their building, he saw his friend Julius sitting on the top step, elbows on his knees and chin in his hands.

'Couldn't get back to sleep,' stated Julius and then, as Stefan got closer, 'Phew! You stink!'

'No water,' said Stefan simply and sat down next to Julius.

'Did the school get hit?' asked Julius hopefully.

'No such luck, just some houses,' answered Stefan 'but my mother needs looking after, so maybe I can get a day off tomorrow. Do you think your mother would let you miss school?'

Julius said he would do his best to persuade her and wanted to know what Stefan had in mind. Stefan was always up to something; he loved to take things apart and invent new ways of putting them back together. His father was always making and repairing things, so there were plenty of tools around.

'Well, we could start by collecting some of the burned-out incendiary bombs. There's usually some snuffed-out magnesium left,' said Stefan nonchalantly. This was the kind of activity that Julius was not so keen on. Stefan's other friend Manfred was into dangerous experiments – Julius was more timid. Stefan put this down to the fact that Julius' father had suffered from wounds from the 1914-18 war.

'How about foraging in the forest; the blackberries are just ripening,' suggested Julius, hoping to distract Stefan's thoughts from more daunting activities.

'Ok, Mama likes blackberries – but I'll keep my eye out for incendiaries anyway,' replied Stefan. He was determined to try out some new experiments, but accepted that he would have to wait until he was with his friend Manfred.

Julius got up to go. 'You'll need a good scrub before you get into bed – or you'll be dreaming about sleeping in a pig sty all night,' he said laughing as he let himself into his apartment. Stefan looked at his hands and the splashes on his shoes. He took the shoes off and left them in the kitchen to be cleaned in the morning. Then he tiptoed quietly into the long narrow bathroom and washed his hands as thoroughly as he could in the cold water.

Stefan went back into the bedroom to sit with his mother.

'I think I fell on the baby,' said his mother 'but please don't mention it to anyone Stefan — only your father needs to know.'

'Yes Mama. Would you like me to look for blackberries tomorrow? Julius said they're just ripening,' said Stefan hopefully.

'Blackberries would be lovely,' replied his mother as she began to drift back to sleep.

Stefan began to undress, putting his clothes neatly out of the way and putting his night shirt back on. It was nearly dawn so he wouldn't get much sleep. He planned to fall asleep thinking about walking in the forest with the scent of pine needles underfoot. The air outside was still pungent with smoke.

Speaking in a soft whisper, his mother called across 'Close the window Stefan.'

Chapter Two

Stefan's baby brother Peter was born on a cold day in November. It seemed to Stefan that his mother had been in labour for a very long time. Everyone was relieved to hear the baby's first cries and the midwife announce that it was a baby boy. His father had gone straight in to check on Mama and the baby. When he came out of the bedroom some minutes later he beckoned to Stefan.
'Stefan, come here please, I need to talk to you,' said his father in a subdued voice.
'There is something wrong with your brother's feet. Don't upset your Mama by talking about it, and I don't want you talking about it to your friends, do you understand?' he continued. Stefan promised that he would say nothing and went in to look at the little bundle lying at the side of his exhausted mother. The tiny baby was swaddled in a blanket and he could just see a tiny crumpled pink face.

Peter was born with twisted feet because of the fall. There were constant visits from the authorities who kept asking if there was anything else wrong with him, or an inherited weakness in the family. Stefan's mother was terrified that the authorities would take the baby away. No one in the family spoke about it. Neighbours said nothing, but they all knew what happened to children who were disabled in any way. Baby Peter needed constant attention, so Stefan's parents had little time to spare for his older brother.

School carried on in spite of the air raids. Stefan got up early, sharpened his slate pencil on the edge of the sandstone kitchen sink, found his shoes and set off. He didn't have far to walk to school, he didn't even have to cross the road. His friend Manfred was waiting by the entrance to the old building that was used for the boys.
'Have you got time to go into the forest this afternoon?' asked Manfred, 'I don't have any chores today,' he continued hopefully.
'I might have to look after Peter,' said Stefan as they trooped into school, 'but we could always take him with us.'

Their first lesson was maths. At eleven o'clock, they were all sent into the yard for a break. They marched in a circle on the tarmac while the girls, who had their lessons in the new building, marched in a circle in the opposite direction.
'I found some old strips of leather in the workshop,' said Manfred in a muffled voice. He had just stuffed some bread and cheese into his mouth.
'Big enough to sit on?' asked Stefan eagerly, 'could we use them for a swing seat?'
'Do you have any strong rope?' asked Manfred, his mouth still stuffed full.
'I think I saw some old rope in a burnt-out house on the Post Road; we can take a

look this afternoon,' replied Stefan hurriedly as they trooped back inside for a history lesson.

Later that day, Stefan and Manfred set out for the forest on the old Post Road. Stefan was pulling his grandmother's ladder-wagon — so called because the sides of the cart looked as if they were made from two ladders laid on their sides. The cart was a good size, big enough for a ten-year-old to sit in, but not too heavy to pull along flat ground. Manfred had already loaded the strips of leather into the cart.
'How much rope is there?' asked Manfred, 'will there be enough space in the cart?'
'Easily, I'm more worried about it not being long enough to reach a good strong high branch,' replied Stefan doubtfully. 'Mama has asked me to collect some firewood while we're there — the axe is under that old sack,' continued Stefan, 'it might be useful if we need to cut the rope.'

Manfred felt a little uneasy about the axe. He knew that people weren't allowed to cut any wood in the forest, only collect what had fallen.
'Just keep it hidden, I don't want to get into any trouble,' he whispered to Stefan and found himself looking over his shoulder to see if anyone was watching them.
Stefan shrugged his shoulders, 'Grandmother and I bring the axe all the time — I'm not

scared,' he said flippantly, but he checked that it was covered up all the same.

When they reached the burned-out remains of the house, Stefan pulled the cart up close to the façade that was still standing eerily by itself. He didn't want to leave his grandmother's cart unattended. He told Manfred to stay with the cart while he went in to see if he could find the rope, hoping that no one else had scavenged it in the meantime. It took him about fifteen minutes to search through the rubble; someone had been there and moved things around. When he did eventually find it, just an end was visible. It took another five minutes to pull it free from under the wreckage. By the time he got back to the cart, Manfred was looking very anxious.
'I thought you might have got buried under a collapsing wall or something – it's really dangerous to go into a bombed-out house – they're always going on about it at school,' he complained. But he soon brightened when he saw the long rope and saw how strong it was.
'Do you think we'll be able to find a tree that we can climb?' wondered Manfred, 'it's going to be pretty heavy to carry up.'
'I could tie it round my waist before climbing up,' offered Stefan.

They coiled the rope as best they could and lifted it into the cart. They each took hold of one of the handle bars to pull the cart. It was only about a ten-minute walk to the edge of the forest.

'We've got a couple of hours before it gets dark,' said Stefan 'if we collect some dry wood while we're looking for a good tree we won't have to do it later.' Stefan began collecting wood straight away while Manfred pulled the cart. They had collected more than enough before Manfred called out excitedly.

'There! Look, that one up there! It's perfect!' Stefan followed Manfred's gaze and saw what he was pointing at. The branch wasn't as high as Stefan would have liked, but it looked very sturdy and strong. Not only that, the lower branches were positioned in such a way that it would be easy for him to climb.

'I'll get the rope up first,' said Stefan 'and then we can think about how to attach the leather pieces.'

One end of the rope was tied around Stefan's waist so that both his hands were free. He needed a leg up from Manfred to reach the first branch, but from there it was quite easy. Once he had reached the biggest branch he sat sideways on it and, holding onto another branch higher up, shuffled along about half a metre.

'Go a bit further,' called Manfred 'otherwise we'll just keep swinging into the tree.'

Keeping a tight grip on the higher branch, Stefan shuffled further along. He looked down and his legs felt a bit wobbly.

'This'll do,' he shouted down to Manfred. Then Stefan realised that to undo the rope from his waist he would have to let go of the branch above him. Feeling rather foolish, he shuffled back towards the trunk of the tree. He leant his back against the trunk and wedged his feet against two side branches for stability while he untied the rope. This time Stefan lay on his front along the branch and edged slowly forward like an inch worm, carrying the rope in one hand and hanging on to the overhanging branch with the other.
'Hurry up!' called Manfred 'or there'll be no time to try it out.'
Stefan grunted and set about securing the rope before shuffling back along the branch.
'Wait till I get down," he shouted in excitement and scrambled back down the tree.
Manfred had already tied the leather strips into a sort of platform – you couldn't really sit on it.
'I think we'll just have to stand on it,' he said disappointedly.
'You can go first – I'll give you a leg up,' offered Stefan.
Manfred put his foot into Stefan's hands and reached up. He grabbed the rope and managed to trap the rope between both feet just above the platform.
'Give me a push – let's see how high we can go,' he shouted down to Stefan.

Stefan grabbed his legs and gave him a hard push. It swung beautifully under the branch and began to twist at the same time.

'Woohoo!' yelled Manfred 'give me another push!'

After a few minutes, Manfred's hands were getting tired and he dropped to the ground.

'Your turn,' he said and gave Stefan a leg up.

'Hold tight!' Manfred yelled up at Stefan, as he took hold of the bottom of the rope beneath the platform, and ran with it as fast as he could in one direction before letting go. It was better than a push; Stefan found himself swinging and twirling higher than Manfred had gone. For a few moments he had a feeling of exhilaration before he heard an ominous creaking sound. Looking up at the branch, he could see the bark beginning to split where the branch joined the trunk of the tree. The branch they had chosen must have been rotten inside and was breaking under the strain. Stefan braced himself for a fall.

'Watch out!' called Manfred 'the branch is breaking!'

There was a horrible cracking and groaning sound as the branch broke away. Stefan clung to the rope trying to decide if it would be safer to jump. But the branch didn't snap, instead it gradually peeled away from the trunk, lowering Stefan gently to the ground. It was disappointing but at least he wasn't hurt.

'Oh well, it was fun while it lasted,' said Manfred consolingly.
'And we have a good piece of rope still,' said Stefan untying the rope from the broken branch and stowing it back in the cart.

The sky was already beginning to darken and the boys could feel the temperature beginning to drop. They headed back for home at a brisk pace. As they emerged from the edge of the forest, air raid sirens could be heard beginning their wail over Mannheim. The boys ran the rest of the way, with the ladder-wagon clattering along behind them. They parted at Stefan's house. Stefan quickly parked the cart in the back yard and ran upstairs to look for Mama and Peter. Mama had bundled Peter into some warm blankets and was obviously waiting for Stefan.
'Quickly, into the house cellar – no time to get to the shelter,' she instructed him without wasting any words.
They ran down the stairs into the cellar with the washing copper, bottled fruit and firewood. Julius, his sister and mother were already there.
'Where's Papa?' asked Stefan. His father would normally be home by this time.
'This raid is earlier than usual,' answered Mama, 'he might've been called out to help already - you know he has responsibilities.'

Stefan knew that it would be a long night and that supper might be a long time coming, if at all. He went to sit with Julius and his sister, and told them about the rope swing and the broken branch.

'Can I come next time?' asked Julius.

'If it's OK with your Mama,' replied Stefan, knowing that Julius' mother was more protective of her son than his own Mama. He was very glad that he was allowed to play in the forest so often.

Several hours later, before the all clear had sounded, Stefan's father suddenly appeared, coming down the cellar stairs.

'The Lindenhof is on fire,' he stated, 'the authorities have sent trucks to fetch people to help.'

Stefan had heard of that part of the city, it was where the wealthy families lived. He scrambled into the back of the truck with his father and other people from the neighbourhood who were going to help. By the time they arrived, most of the fires had been put out and people were already searching for belongings in the rubble. Stefan found himself near a distraught woman who asked him to help her save her clothes and jewellery. There was a lovely glider on a shelf. He wanted to rescue it from the flames.

'I'll just get that glider,' he told the woman.

'No, there isn't time; the building could collapse at any moment! Please, I need my clothes," she called back anxiously.

Stefan managed to get to a wardrobe and bundle up some clothes for the woman. He wasn't able to save the glider and sadly watched as it was consumed in the flames.

'People need their clothes Stefan,' his father said consolingly as they climbed back into the truck to go home. 'You've been a great help here; that woman will be very grateful,' he continued with pride in his son's efforts. The helpers were tired and covered in dust and ashes; nobody spoke on the journey home.

By the time they got back to the apartment, Stefan was feeling very hungry; he hadn't had anything to eat since breakfast because he forgot to take his mid-morning snack to school.
As they mounted the stairs to their apartment they could hear the baby beginning to cry. Stefan knew that he would have to find his own supper while his mother took care of Peter. He managed to find a chunk of rye bread and the end of a sausage to eat and went into the bedroom. The baby was still crying. Stefan knew that his twisted feet hurt Peter especially when he needed changing. His mother was looking anxious.
'I don't want the neighbours to hear Peter crying,' she said in a tearful voice 'close the window Stefan.'

Chapter Three

'Stefan!' called his mother 'can you go down and fetch the sausage soup from Mr Willmann please, I'm busy with the baby'.
The house where Stefan's family lived was owned by Mr Willmann the butcher. He was known as a very good butcher, who had learned his trade in London before the Great War. He lived on the ground floor that included the shop and his 'sausage kitchen'. Every Friday when the sausages had been cooked he would sell the left-over stock, calling it sausage soup. Sometimes one of the sausages would burst during cooking, making the soup extra tasty. Stefan's mother would add a few vegetables or oats to make a cheap but nourishing meal. It was Friday, and Stefan could smell the delicious odour of the sausages being prepared as it drifted up towards their balcony window.
'Yes Mama,' he called back and went downstairs. It was the end of November, and the very large horse chestnut tree in the yard opposite had already shed most of its leaves. The wind had blown the leaves into all the nooks and crannies and some had blown under the door into the entrance hall. Stefan had to go out of the house and round to the shop entrance on the main street. As he did so, a gust of wind caught a pile of leaves and whisked them up into his face so that for a moment he couldn't see. When he had brushed the leaves from

his eyes he found himself looking into the face of a boy he hadn't seen before. He looked as if he was younger than Stefan.

'Hello,' said Stefan, in what he hoped was a friendly voice, 'I haven't seen you before.'

'We've only just moved in, we're on the top floor,' said the boy, 'my name is David.'

'I'm Stefan. I'm just going into the shop to fetch some sausage soup; do you want to come with me?' asked Stefan, not wasting any time in getting acquainted with a possible new friend.

Together they squeezed into the shop that was packed with women queuing for their sausage rations. The women were all talking at once. One large woman had a particularly loud voice.

'How small are you going to make those portions Mr Willmann? Any smaller and we might as well not bother," she complained.

Poor Mr Willmann lost concentration under the harassment, and let out a yelp as he cut his finger. He saw a drop of blood and went rigid, the colour draining from his face. The big knife he had been using slipped out of his fingers and fell to the floor with a clatter. Then the big strong butcher dropped as if his legs had been taken from him. He fainted and fell to the floor, crashing into pots that were sent flying as he went down. The women in the shop all began shouting and arguing about what to do. Stefan took hold of David and ushered him hurriedly out of the shop.

'What happened?' asked David in bewilderment.

'Oh Mr Willmann can't stand the sight of blood after being in a road accident; a bit inconvenient for a butcher! C'mon, we'll come back later,' said Stefan unruffled by the event. They went back outside into the chilly November air and ran back into the yard just as the wind scooped up a pile of leaves and hurled it towards them.

'Would you like to come with me to fetch some honey from our bees?' asked David.

'I'd rather go and play,' said Stefan. 'Can't you do that tomorrow when there's no school?' he continued.

'We don't work on Saturdays,' said David rather shyly.

'Why not?' asked Stefan curiously.

'We're Seventh Day Adventists,' explained David. Stefan had no idea what that meant, but he had a suspicion that it might mean trouble for the family. He told David not to tell anyone else, but said that he would talk to his father.

'He'll know what to do for the best,' he said confidently 'my father has responsibilities you know.'

The two boys spent the next few hours together. David fed the bees and collected honey, and a very puffy face, while Stefan watched from a safe distance.

'What about the Youth Folk?' asked Stefan 'It's on Saturday mornings – will you be able to go? It's compulsory – the police can make

you. You can go with me. We have to do marching, and sometimes a bit of history, but mostly we play games in the forest'.
David thought his parents would let him go. He didn't think it counted as work.
'I'd better go and get that soup for Mama,' sighed Stefan, 'I expect Mr Willman has recovered by now.'
The boys agreed to meet in the morning so that they could go together to the Youth Folk and Stefan obediently went into the butcher's shop to collect the soup for his mother. Later that evening, Stefan told his father about David's family.
'They're Seventh Day Adventists Papa, does that matter?' he asked.
'I think it'll be best if they don't tell people,' he replied, 'I wouldn't want them to find themselves in any trouble, I am sure they're a good honest family. Take David with you to the Youth Folk tomorrow, it'll allay suspicion. I have a busy day tomorrow; the orphanage needs some replacement roof tiles and I promised I'd get them,' he continued.
Next morning, true to his word, Stefan called for David. Stefan was wearing a scarf and an arm band, but no proper uniform - it was too expensive. He checked that David's shoes were clean and properly fastened and then measured the length of his shorts.
'No knee ticklers,' he told David, 'they have to be a hand width above the knee. Don't worry, they'll give you an arm band — you

need one for the war games, if it gets torn, you're dead,' he explained.

The boys spent the morning with a lot of other boys playing war games and practising their marching — they weren't very good at it. The leader, an older boy from the Hitler Youth, kept shouting at them 'left is where the thumb is on the right!' But the games were fun and the forest was the best kind of playground.

When it was all over, Stefan was in no hurry to go home. David had to get back to his family because it was their special day of the week. Stefan walked him to the end of the road and then headed back into the forest.

One of Stefan's favourite pastimes was making fireworks. After an air raid, there would always be a few incendiary bombs that had landed on the sandy forest floor and stopped burning before all the magnesium had been used up. Today was no exception, after about an hour of searching he found two bombs. One was completely burnt out, but the other looked as if a lot was still usable. It was about half-a metre in length and weighed about the same as a large cat, so he was able to carry it quite easily. It looked a bit like the end of an over-sized pencil with its hexagonal shape.

At home, as usual, his mother was busy with the baby and he knew his father would be pre-occupied with the orphanage roof. Stefan was allowed to use his father's tools to prepare his home-made fireworks. He used a hacksaw to remove the steel ends of the bomb and get to the unused section that was made of solid magnesium alloyed with some sodium. Then he filed some of the magnesium into a powder. Next, he ground up some of the purple tablets that his mother bought from the pharmacist as a disinfectant and mixed it with the magnesium powder. Some time ago, he had discovered some paper in an old book that rolled up into the perfect tube for his bangers. It was very thick paper from an old Napoleonic book that he had found. One of his great uncles had served under The Grand Duchess of Baden at the palace in Mannheim, and the book had found its way into Stefan's home. The paper made a good crack when it exploded.

Stefan rolled up a page from the book and sealed one end with a small piece of wire. He carefully poured his powdered mixture into the paper tube. Next he took some paper string – it was the only kind of string you could get because of rationing – unravelled it and flattened it out. He still had some homemade gunpowder left from his last experiment, made from salt peter granules, sulphur powder that he got from the kind old gentleman who owned the pharmacy across the road and home-made charcoal. Stefan moulded the paper string into a kind of trough and poured in a thin line of gunpowder. He pushed one end of the string into the open end of the tube and then sealed it with wire.

Stefan didn't think it would be fair to set the banger off by himself without sharing it with someone, so he ran up to the top floor and called for David. David watched in awe as Stefan carefully carried his home-made banger into the garden. He watched in some horror as Stefan lit the end of the paper string that acted as a fuse and stood back to watch the effect of his handiwork.

The firework exploded with a tremendous crack and there was a flash of beautiful white light! David stood for a moment in shock and then let out a whoop of joy. But his pleasure was short-lived. His father, convinced that there had been a terrible accident, came running to the scene and discovering that it was only a school-boy experiment scolded them both and took David back up to their apartment. It was some weeks before he would again be allowed to go anywhere with Stefan.

Stefan's mother wasn't happy either.

'You should be thinking about how to make yourself useful,' she admonished, 'not fooling about with dangerous chemicals. You can take Peter for a walk, he could do with some fresh air,' she continued.

Stefan was very happy to be asked to go out even if it was beginning to get dark. He put Peter in his moulded-cardboard pram; made sure he was warmly wrapped up, and set off down the Post Road in the direction of the forest. He was already planning his next firework experiment. He wondered what it would look like if he threw it off the top of a building and how long he would have to wait after lighting the fuse before throwing it in the air.

He felt very fortunate that his father was so tolerant of his experiments and allowed him the use of his tools. Just as he began thinking of his father, his father appeared out of a building about ten metres away. He was carrying a tool box and looked very tired.

'Papa!' called Stefan and ran to meet him. 'What've you been mending?' he asked.

'Mrs Braun needed help with her plumbing. She is a widow with no sons. You know I have responsibilities in the community,' replied Stefan's father. 'The trouble is that everyone expects me to be able to find materials for repairs. There isn't enough for all and I have to choose – I have to decide who needs them most – and some people aren't happy with that,' he continued sadly. 'What have you been up to today?'

Stefan told him about his fireworks and how bright and beautiful the flash was. He also told him about how David's father had been upset and banned David from playing with him.

'They're good people,' said his father 'I'm sure he only meant it for the best. But you must be careful about what you say to people, I've already heard some of the neighbours making comments about David's family being different. I'll try to warn them not to be too outspoken — it isn't safe.'

Stefan's father looked up into the sky and shivered.

'It's a clear night, it'll be cold,' he stated as he took hold of the push chair, turned it round and headed for home.

Later that evening, after a supper of left-over sausage soup and thick pieces of rye bread, they could hear the sound of David's family singing hymns accompanied by an old harmonium.

'The neighbours might hear,' said his father softly so as not to wake Peter, 'close the window Stefan.'

'Mama, the Hitler Youth are going to be making wooden toys to give to the poor children for Christmas. Please can I go and help?' Stefan asked his mother.

'Check with Papa before you make any commitments,' she answered breathlessly, fighting against a strong north-easterly wind.

Stefan and his mother were hurrying home in the gathering gloom of a cold December evening. Peter was snugly wrapped in blankets in his cardboard pram to keep out the bitter chill, but Stefan's legs, bare below his shorts, were red from the cold. It was a Thursday, so Stefan knew it wouldn't be sausage soup for supper, but he had that to look forward to tomorrow. He was looking forward to tomorrow for another reason as well; it would be St Nikolaus Day and that meant chocolates!

As they rounded the corner of Mannheim Street, they could see a new sign being painted on the big gate that led to a house that used to belong to a Jewish family. The sign had the initials of the government in huge letters. Stefan tried making the letters into a word; it sounded silly, so he began laughing.

'Hush,' cautioned his mother warily as a military car emerged from the gateway. At the same time they saw a woman coming towards them; it was Dr Neumark. She was a particular friend of Stefan's mother. She had helped the family when Stefan had suffered appendicitis and saved his life. But as they approached, Dr Neumark put her fingers to her lips, motioned to them not to stop and hurried past. Stefan could see that his mother was upset and frightened. They finished their short journey in an uneasy silence.

Before supper Stefan had to practice his piano pieces. A few years ago, his father had insisted that he learned to play the piano. They had bought the piano from a widow and there had been a pile of sheet music that came with it. Stefan's Aunt Anna had a very beautiful old piano that she played, and it was Aunt Anna that had persuaded Stefan's father to buy a piano. There always seemed to be music in Stefan's home; his father played the mandolin and guitar, and his mother, who had a wonderful soprano voice, was always singing. Stefan obediently played through his scales and arpeggios and then practised the piece he had been asked to learn by his teacher Miss Oest. His father would take him to his piano lesson tomorrow evening after he had come home from work.

As he was getting ready for bed, Stefan heard his father come home and go into the kitchen to speak to his mother.
'It's Dr Neumark's husband. He's been run over and killed,' he told her.
'Deliberately?' she questioned.

'They're Jews,' he stated simply, giving her the answer.

'They're our friends,' she replied vehemently.

Stefan fell asleep to the sound of his mother softly weeping for her friends.

After school the next day, Stefan ran up the stairs to their apartment and burst through the door with excitement.

'Julius has invited me next door, and he said that St Nikolaus is coming. Can I go please?' he asked his mother breathlessly.

'Of course you can,' replied his mother, 'just as soon as you have changed out of your school clothes and scrubbed your face and hands.'

Stefan threw his school satchel into a corner and hurriedly changed his clothes. He went into the bathroom and lathered up some soap and began to scrub his hands and nails with a small stiff brush. Then he put soap on his flannel and washed his face and neck, and behind the ears. Just to make sure, he scrubbed his knees as well. He knew that St Nikolaus would check that he was clean before he would hand over any chocolates. Next, he carefully polished his shoes, knowing that these would be checked as well.

Stefan knocked on the door to Julius' apartment and shuffled impatiently as he waited for someone to open it. It was Anneliese who opened the door and smiled shyly up at Stefan. Julius squeezed past her and took hold of Stefan's arm, pulling him into the living room.

'Hurry up,' he said excitedly, 'you've been ages, what've you been doing all this time?'

'I had to make sure I was clean,' replied Stefan, 'you know what St Nikolaus is like, it's chocolates I want, not the birch!'

They didn't have long to wait before St Nikolaus arrived at the door. He wore a full-length red robe over what looked like a long white dress. On his head he wore a tall red hat like a Bishop, and he had a long flowing beard. In one hand he held a birch broom for naughty children, and in the other a large and heavy sack.

Both of Julius' parents were there, proudly standing behind the well-scrubbed children. They stood in a line and the boys stood to attention as if on parade. St Nikolaus looked them over, inspecting the backs of their necks, their knees, fingernails, hands and finally their shoes.

'Have they been good children? Do they deserve good things?' he asked Julius' parents.

'Well, they've all been doing their chores and they're undoubtedly clean at the moment,' replied Julius' mother to the children's great relief.

'What about any special deeds?' asked St Nikolaus.

At this point Julius stepped forward and recited a poem. It was quite long and Stefan had trouble not fidgeting. St Nikolaus smiled broadly and was clearly pleased with the poem.

'Any other special deeds?' he asked, looking at the other children.

Anneliese stepped forward and sang a short folk song in a shy husky voice.

St Nikolaus patted her on the head.

'Any others?' he asked, looking directly at Stefan.

Stefan felt rather hot under the collar. He had a good singing voice, but Julius hadn't warned him so he wasn't prepared, and he could never remember any poems. Instead he looked down at the floor and shook his head.

'In that case, let's see what we can find in the sack,' said St Nikolaus in a kindly voice as he emptied the contents onto the carpet. St Nikolaus sorted the contents into three piles. Stefan's pile was noticeably smaller than the others. Each of the children had a chocolate model of St Nikolaus that stood about twenty centimetres high. In addition there were various sweets and chocolate-covered biscuits.

The children were allowed to eat some of the biscuits straight away but told to save their chocolate St Nikolaus until after supper. Stefan had a very healthy appetite and was quite sure that no amount of chocolate would have spoiled his supper, but he obediently contented himself with the biscuits. He didn't stay long after this. It was too late to go out to play and Julius was needed to help his mother.

Stefan let himself back into his apartment, carefully carrying his chocolate St Nikolaus to show to his mother. She was in the kitchen busy changing Peter's nappy. He had nothing on except the plaster on his deformed feet.
'Stefan, watch the baby for a moment please I need to stir the stew before it burns on the bottom of the pan, and don't let him fall off,' warned his mother.
Stefan stood by the side of the table to watch Peter. Then he noticed that there seemed to be something wriggling underneath him. Peering more closely he saw little white worms coming out of the baby onto the clean nappy! Stefan's curiosity got the better of him and he picked up one of the worms and watched it squirm between his finger and thumb. His mother came back at this moment.
'Stefan, put that down and scrub your hands this instant,' she scolded 'and make sure you use the nail brush, or we'll all have worms!' she continued 'then go and get a cucumber from the garden, he'll be able to eat some mashed up – that'll get rid of the nasty little beasts.'

It wasn't long before his father came home to take Stefan to his piano lesson. Stefan carried his music book, and since it was already dark his father carried his tin torch. It was still early evening and there were other people about outside, mostly hurrying home to get out of the chill winter air. They could see Sister Karolina coming towards them, head bent low against the bitter wind. She had been Stefan's teacher when he was in kindergarten and was always pleased to see him. Her face lit up with a beaming smile when she saw Stefan.

'Where are you off to in this cold wind?' she asked him.

'Papa is taking me to my piano lesson,' he answered politely. Next to his parents and Peter, Stefan loved Sister Karolina more than anyone.

'Perhaps one day I will hear you play the piano, but alas we do not have one anymore,' replied the Sister sadly. Then she turned to Stefan's father and put her hands together as if in prayer.

'We know that food is always in short supply, but somehow the usual donations to the church orphanage have not been reaching us. Some of the girls are showing signs of malnutrition.'

She took hold of one of Stefan's father's hands and looked deep into his eyes.

'I know you will help if you can,' she said simply 'God bless you.'

She pulled her cloak tightly about her, smiled once more at Stefan and continued on her way.

They carried on in silence. Stefan's father seemed deep in thought. It wasn't long before they arrived at the block where Miss Oest had her apartment.

'Your mother would want me to help the Sisters,' said his father, 'if I go now there may be some supplies that can be redistributed. Do you think you can find your own way home in the dark?' he asked.

Stefan was quite happy walking in the dark; he could find his way home in the forest at night where there were no streets or houses.

'Of course Papa, don't worry about me.'

His father laughed and strode away into the darkness.

Miss Oest's apartment had not yet been damaged in the air raids. It was in an elegant building and her apartment was richly furnished. Most importantly, she owned a beautifully ornate grand piano that Stefan was allowed to play on when his teacher held little concerts for her students. At other times they played on her upright piano. Stefan was ushered into the comfortable apartment by his smiling teacher. There was a lively fire in the grate and the window was open a little so that the fire could draw.

'Where's your father?' questioned Miss Oest, 'he's usually with you.'

'Oh he's gone to redistribute supplies,' replied Stefan quoting his father's words, 'he has responsibilities you know.'

Miss Oest just nodded as they went towards the upright piano. Stefan mechanically went through his scales and arpeggios. Next he played the piece that he had been learning. His teacher seemed pleased with his progress, making a few suggestions to improve his fingering.

'I'm glad to see that you cleaned your hands before you came,' said Miss Oest, 'I half expected them to be covered in chocolate – did St Nikolaus visit you this evening?'

'Oh yes, I had piles of stuff,' exaggerated Stefan with enthusiasm.

Miss Oest changed the subject back to the lesson.

'You've just been playing a piece by Mozart, what can you remember about him?' she asked.

'He was a child prodigy,' replied Stefan.

'Yes and what was his connection with Mannheim?' probed Miss Oest.

'He performed in the Mannheim Palace and met his wife here,' answered Stefan confidently.

'Good. Now you're going to learn a piece by another composer who has a connection with Mannheim, and he was also a child prodigy. His name is Mendelssohn. His son was a chemist who founded a chemical factory that now owns the Aniline factory in Mannheim-Ludwigshafen. I shall play through the piece first so that you can hear it.'

Stefan got up and stood at the side of the piano while Miss Oest settled herself on the stool. She paused, and then in a subdued voice explained to Stefan that Mendelssohn's music had been banned. His family had been Jewish.

'Please, before I begin,' she said softly 'would you close the window Stefan.'

Chapter Five

Stefan staggered, momentarily confused. As he looked along the street it seemed to be swaying. Or was it him that was swaying? He reached out to his friend Manfred and grabbed his arm.

'There's something wrong,' he said, 'I feel dizzy, sort of tipping sideways.'

Manfred shrugged him off 'what are you doing?' he asked 'trying to get out of school? It won't work you know.'

Stefan steadied himself and looked again. Gradually, he realised what he was looking at. It wasn't him that was swaying, or the street. It was one building, or rather the remaining façade of a four-story sandstone building. He grabbed at Manfred again, this time dragging him back along the street. There wasn't time to check back over his shoulder.

'Run!' he shouted at Manfred who responded to the urgency in Stefan's voice.

As they ran there was a rush of air and clouds of dust swept past them. The rumble of the tumbling stone seemed to come up through the ground under their running feet. They ran into a side street and threw themselves with their backs against a sturdy wall. Stefan felt himself shaking, his legs wobbled and in his relief, he began to laugh. He slid down with his back against the wall and found himself sitting against Manfred who was taking great gulping breaths of air.

'That won't work either,' gasped Manfred as they both laughed in relief at their narrow escape.

The war had already dragged on for three years and little Peter was nearly two. Stefan's twelfth birthday had been in the summer, and he had started at the high school in Mannheim that September. It seemed most unfair to all the boys that the school never got hit in the air raids. There was one teacher in particular that all the boys hated. He taught history and he was very strict. The boys even planned ways to get rid of him. Stefan couldn't see the point of learning history, or even going to school with all that was going on around them. Many of the boys felt the same way. But Stefan liked the head of music; he was a good musician. He had been injured, and so could no longer serve as a soldier, but still wanted to play his part. He helped with a special choir that sang for the troops and their families.
Because Stefan played the piano, could read music and sing, he was allowed to join these special events. He was given vouchers to get a proper uniform — they were good clothes and Stefan felt proud to be wearing them. There was to be a special memorial service for the families of war heroes, and Stefan found himself part of a very large choir together with a number of other schools. They had to practise singing in a large hall in Mannheim.

When the day came, all the children gathered in the hall with the troops, their families and invited celebrities. There was nowhere to sit. Everyone had to stand still and not move. Stefan found himself wanting to fidget, his legs started to ache. He couldn't see much because there were so many people standing in front of him. People were getting hot and the air became stifling. They began playing stirring music over the loudspeaker and some of the women began to cry. Stefan felt uncomfortable. Then a man stood up and started shouting hysterically, ranting about their fallen heroes who had sacrificed themselves so courageously. Stefan couldn't really understand how dying made anyone a hero, and felt guilty about not feeling the way everyone seemed to expect him to. He just wanted to sit down on the floor but dare not cause a fuss, and besides there was no space. Then a girl nearby fainted. She just dropped to the floor. Nobody did anything; they just left her there on the floor. Others fainted too, but the man just kept going on and on. To Stefan it felt as if it would never end. Eventually it did finish and Stefan could escape into the cool fresh air. He was glad to get away from all the grief and emotion, and he did get to keep the smart uniform.
The hall was bombed shortly afterwards and couldn't be used again. Then at last, the school was hit and Stefan could spend his time helping his mother at home or his grandmother in the garden. He was often sent

into the forest to collect wood or mushrooms. His grandmother had shown him where to look for edible mushrooms and how to hide a patch so that others would not take them before they had a chance to grow to a good size. Late one afternoon, Stefan's mother sent him on one of these errands.

'I need some mushrooms for our supper Stefan. Take a bag from the cupboard and see what you can find. You know what to look for,' she said 'and be careful of the leaves,' she continued.

'Yes Mama, you needn't remind me about the leaves, Grandma tells me how poisonous they are every time we go into the forest,' he replied.

Stefan got a bag out of a cupboard in the corner of the kitchen. It was a shopping bag made of string; it looked like a folded fishing net with rope handles. The holes were small enough so that good-sized mushrooms wouldn't fall out. He put his boots on and then went next door to call for Julius to see if he could go with him.

'I'm sorry,' said Julius 'Mama needs my help, especially since Papa...'

Julius didn't finish the sentence. His voice trailed away and ended on a sob.

'I understand,' said Stefan in a quiet voice, 'do you think your Mama would like me to collect some mushrooms for her as well?' he continued.

'I'll just go and ask,' muttered Julius as he went off into the kitchen. Anneliese appeared at the door.

'I'd go with you,' she said shyly 'but it's already late and Mama wouldn't let me, but you can borrow this bag if you like,' she added handing Stefan a small leather bag with a long strap attached. Stefan thought the bag would be too small for mushrooms but he liked the bag so he slung it over his shoulder and thanked her. Julius came back.

'She said if you can find a fat hen she'd be very grateful. I have to take the big pot to the blacksmith to be mended. Maybe I'll see you later.' Julius shrugged his shoulders and shut the door.

Stefan knew that a fat hen was the name local people used for a particularly large white mushroom that was good for cooking. He also knew exactly where to find one. He set off alone down the Post Road and into the familiar forest.

He went straight to the place where he knew there would be at least one good-sized white fat hen. He removed the twigs and leaves that he had piled over the patch of mushrooms and measured the two largest. They were both big enough, but he thought it was a shame that the smaller one couldn't have been left another few days to grow. Next he went in search of some parasol mushrooms. True they had poisonous leaves, but the mushrooms themselves could be eaten without cooking. They had a lovely crisp nutty flavour. It took about half-an-hour of hunting in the undergrowth but he found a good patch. He ate a few, being careful of the leaves, and then decided to pick the rest and put them in the bag that Anneliese had lent to him. They would make a tasty late-night snack. He always seemed to be hungry at night nowadays. He would often wake in the early hours, even when there were no air raids, feeling ravenously hungry.

He had a bit of a hunt around for some stone mushrooms but couldn't find any. The light was just beginning to fade. It had been a gloriously sunny afternoon but the sun, glowing red, was heading towards the horizon. He realised that he must have been in the forest for longer than he had planned. His mother would be cross if he didn't get home in time for the mushrooms to be prepared for supper.

Before he had taken more than two steps he heard the disturbing sound of the air raid siren winding up to its wailing pitch that pierced the still air. Stefan immediately broke into a run; he knew all the short cuts and headed in the direction of home as fast as he could go.

The air defences had been positioned at the edge of the forest. The soldiers operating the batteries of anti-aircraft guns were firing like madmen. Stefan looked up into the sky. He could see the marker lights that looked like Christmas trees dropped by the RAF to mark out where they were to drop their bombs.

He could hear the first wave of bombers approaching. The noise from the anti-aircraft artillery was deafening, and splinters from the exploding shells began to rain down on the forest. Stefan grabbed at Anneliese's leather bag and used it to cover his head, knowing that the falling shrapnel was more dangerous than the risk of bombs in the forest.
Still running at full speed, Stefan thought about jumping into a bomb crater, reasoning that two bombs were not likely to fall on the same spot. But that wouldn't have protected him from the falling shrapnel that was worse than anything. He remembered a burnt-out house at the edge of the forest and ran towards it. As he reached the surrounding fence, he threw both bags over first. Then he jumped up and caught hold of the top edge and hauled himself over. Grabbing both bags he scrambled over the ruins and found the entrance to the basement, slipping down the steps in his haste. He sat on the floor and took great gulps of air to try to recover his breath. The muscles in his legs and arms ached; he felt as if he had been stretched on a rack. He lay flat on the hard floor in the dark and listened as the first wave of bombers went over.

After a while, he got up and had a look around. The basement was quite large with an open space and still in good condition. There were some empty bottles lying around, but not much else. He listened and waited and nibbled one of the parasol mushrooms. Then he went up and looked out to where the artillery could be seen. He could see the soldiers trying to put out fires on the roof. But moments later they began firing shells into the air again as a second wave of bombers came over. Stefan hurried back down into the safety of the basement. He knew his mother would be worried but he was safer down here than trying to get back home.

Stefan began to lose track of time, he was in the basement so long. There were five waves of bombers, and in between each wave Stefan looked out to see what was happening with the artillery. There should have been a beautiful sunset, but it was marred by thick smoke rising over Mannheim. Eventually it finished. By this time Stefan had eaten most of the parasol mushrooms – he hoped they wouldn't upset his stomach. He approached the fence ready to climb back over, trying to find the lowest point where he must have climbed over. He couldn't understand how he had got over the fence, it was much too high, and now he couldn't get out. It must have been fear that helped him jump the fence before, but now there was no chance he could jump back over.

Stefan hunted around for things to use to help him escape. In the basement, he found some old wooden shelves. They had obviously been made to fit along one of the walls and would not fit up the stairs in one piece.

Stefan set about breaking the shelving into smaller pieces that he would be able to carry up by himself. To begin with he jumped on the lower slats to break a few off, and then he could use them to lever off some of the slats higher up. He dragged as much of the wood up the stairs as he could break off and leant it against the fence. It wasn't enough, so he dragged some of the rubble across and began to build a kind of mound against the fence, using the wooden slats as a framework. Eventually the mound was high enough for Stefan to be able to scramble back over the fence, clutching both bags. He dropped down on the other side and looked up, again wondering how he could have jumped over it before.

Stefan didn't hurry home. There was no danger now, and he knew his father would be busy organising working parties to put out fires, and distributing food and medical supplies. His mother would be making sure Peter had some supper, even though there were no mushrooms. He knew it would be some time before there would be any supper for him or his father. He slung the leather bag back over his shoulder and carried the other bag loosely in one hand, and he slowly dawdled back home. As he passed the cemetery, a covered horse-drawn wagon turned into the gate just in front of him. Stefan shuddered as a hand slipped from under the cover and momentarily brushed his face. Stefan thought it was curious how bodies shrank when they had been burned.

When Stefan turned the corner, he could see that their apartment was untouched and he breathed a sigh of relief. He slowly climbed the stairs, left his shoes outside the door and went in. His mother, as he had expected, was busy giving Peter his supper.

'Stefan, your father and I have decided that it's time you were evacuated,' said his mother without looking at him.

'With the school; like Walter?' Stefan asked.

'No, Julius' mother has been kind enough to offer to take you to stay on a family farm,' replied his mother.

'With Julius?' asked Stefan hopefully.

'Yes' came the reply.

For once Stefan felt he had something to look forward to; it would be like a long holiday. Outside in the street they heard the clanging sound of the bells of a fire engine. Stefan's mother took Peter's empty dish in one hand and passed her other hand wearily across her brow. With a deep sigh she simply said 'close the window Stefan.'

Part two
Chapter Six

'Watch out! Mind the corners! One more step... nearly there,' called Stefan's Uncle Henry as he reached the last step of the flight of stairs. Uncle Henry and his father had just carried Stefan's piano down from their apartment. They were both strong men but it was hard work and they were damp with sweat.

'I hope they've left enough space on the wagon,' puffed Uncle Henry, 'go and check will you Stefan.'

Stefan ran around to the front of the building where a huge horse-drawn farm wagon was standing in the street. It had already been loaded with all the furniture and belongings of Julius' family. They were moving to the farm where Julius' mother had grown up and had no intention of returning. Stefan was to go with them – he had no idea how long for. He looked up at the wagon.

'Will the piano still fit on?' he asked one of the farm labourers who had come to help with the move.

'Don't worry, we've left enough space and we'll stop it from wobbling about with that mattress your father's already brought down. Is there anything else to go on?' he asked Stefan.

'Just a small suitcase' replied Stefan shouting over the noise of a gossiping crowd that had gathered to watch the move.

Stefan ran back and nearly collided with his father carrying one end of the piano as he rounded the corner of the building.

'There's space Papa,' he said 'shall I go and get my suitcase now?' he asked.

'Yes,' replied his father 'we mustn't keep them waiting – they won't want to be arriving in the dark,' he continued.

Stefan ran back upstairs. Now that it was time to leave he felt a bit strange. His father had insisted that the piano went with them so that he could keep up his practise, and his mattress was going as well. There was an uncomfortable sort of finality about it – almost as if he was moving home with Julius. He put his suitcase in the hallway and went into the kitchen. His mother was busy with Peter as usual.

'Mama, will you come and visit?' asked Stefan trying not to sound anxious.

'Of course, and I'll bring Peter. I'm sure he'd love to see all the farm animals,' she replied briskly. She was going to miss Stefan dreadfully but thought it better not to show her feelings since it might make it harder for him to be brave.

'Now then, off you go and don't dawdle; we don't want to make them wait. I'm sure you'll enjoy life on the farm; the time will fly by and it won't seem long before you see us again,' said his mother encouragingly. She gave him a quick hug and gently ushered him out of the door. She didn't go

downstairs with him; she didn't want to make a scene in front of the neighbours.
Stefan picked up his suitcase and slowly went downstairs. He wondered how long it would be before he would be home again, and if the house would still be there. It would never be the same anyway as Julius wouldn't be there. He briefly wondered who would be moving into the empty apartment.

His suitcase was tucked into a space in the wagon and then Stefan was helped up onto the wooden seat next to Julius. Uncle Henry and his father stood and watched as the wagon began to move off, the horses going at a slow trot. Stefan waved as they rounded a bend and had a final glimpse of his father waving back. It was going to be a long journey, about fifty miles. With the heavily-laden wagon, the horses would take all day to get there.

'I can't believe your father made you bring the piano,' said Julius, 'the neighbours must've thought you were crazy!'
'He wants me to practise every day,' said Stefan, 'he thinks it's really important.'
'I wish I could play the piano,' said Anneliese wistfully, 'but not Chopin or Mozart, I'd want to play songs and then I could sing as well.'
For a moment Stefan felt home-sick as he pictured his father playing the mandolin and both his parents singing. He decided to change the subject.

'Did I ever tell you about my scary great aunt?' he asked Julius, thinking that a good story might while away some of the time.
'No, is this a true story?' asked Julius suspiciously.
'Judge for yourself,' replied Stefan tying to sound intriguing.
'Once upon a time,' began Stefan.
'That's how fairy stories start,' interrupted Anneliese 'so it can't be true.'
'That's how all the best stories start,' said Stefan and then continued.
'When I was about six or seven my father took me on a train journey. We travelled east deep into the mountains and through dark, dense forest. The train slowly wound its way along the steep and gloomy track. The trees were so close together that not a patch of light could be seen on the ground. Peering out of the window I could see the bright eyes of wild animals staring back at me, lurking behind the tall evergreens. Eventually, the train slowed to a stop at Mudau station. Silently, we climbed down from the carriage. There was no one on the platform. It was completely deserted. We stood and watched the train as it sluggishly pulled out of the station. When it was gone, there was an eery silence.'
Anneliese interrupted 'Is it a ghost story?' she asked excitedly.
'Be quiet!' commanded her brother rudely.

Stefan continued 'My father took my hand, and together we walked into the small town. The streets were eerily empty; there was not a soul to be seen or heard. We had to walk out of the town along a very long road. We saw and heard no one.'

'Where was every one?' asked Anneliese 'was it like the Pied Piper of Hamelin, had they all been taken into the mountain?'

'We didn't know,' said Stefan mysteriously 'and we never found out. But we walked deeper and deeper into the cold, dark forest. It seemed to take hours. Finally we could see a clearing in the trees and there was the most enormous gothic castle.'

'What does gothic mean?' asked Anneliese.

'I wish you'd stop interrupting,' complained Julius, 'it means it has towers and turrets, and ghosts as well I should think,' he continued.

'Well it did have turrets and towers,' said Stefan 'and it was very big. But that was not our destination; we had to keep on going. We went right past the castle and even deeper into the forest until we came eventually to a wooden hunting lodge. It had a big wooden door with great iron hinges and an enormous iron ring hanging in the middle. My father took hold of the iron ring and knocked loudly on the door.' At this point Stefan lowered his voice to a whisper.

'We could hear footsteps coming slowly towards the other side of the door. Then we heard heavy iron bolts being pulled back. Then we

could see the door slowly open. We could hear it creaking on its hinges. The door suddenly flew open.'
In a loud voice, that made Anneliese jump, he said 'and we found ourselves looking into the barrel of a shotgun with a fearsome old woman scowling at us!'
He continued in a normal voice 'My father quickly explained that he was her nephew and surely she must remember him. She lowered the gun and peered into his face with her piercing eyes. She nodded slightly, put the gun down and let us in. She was very old and wrinkly, but she seemed pleased to see me and kept patting me on the head.'
'She might have blown your head off!' said Julius
'He's making it up,' said Anneliese 'is that the end?'
'There's a bit more, if you'll stop interrupting,' said Stefan huffily and then continued.
'She gave us some supper, thick slices of rye bread and slices of some strange dark meat. Then the old lady went and got an old wooden box from the bedroom. She told us that for many years she had been the cook up at the castle, and when she retired, the Prince gave her the hunting lodge to live in, the gun to get food, and a golden cross. Then she opened the box and took out a solid gold cross encrusted with rubies. She let me hold it, but it was so heavy I couldn't hold it on my own and Papa had to take it from me. She told us that it came from

Russia and was smuggled out at the time of the Revolution. It was the most beautiful thing I have ever seen.'

'Well where is it now?' asked Anneliese.

'I don't know,' said Stefan 'I haven't been there since.'

'Do you mean it's true?' asked Anneliese.

'Everything except there being no people around, and the bit about Russia,' said Stefan 'I don't remember if she said where it came from – but it could easily be true because the Prince is actually related to the Romanov family.'

'Well I thought you were going to tell a ghost story,' complained Julius 'and it's still hours till we reach the farm.'

The children occupied themselves on the rest of the journey trying to think of games to play, and slowly munching their way through a picnic that Julius' mother had thoughtfully provided. In the late afternoon, they finally arrived in the small farming village of Barbelroth, only a few miles from the French border. To Stefan it had seemed a strange place to choose, but his father had explained that because it was so near to France there was less chance of any bombing.

The houses here were not like Stefan's home. There was no sandstone. They were made with wooden beams and had very steep roofs, four stories high. The wooden shutters at the windows folded outwards instead of rolling up like the ones at home. In the middle of the town there was a hill, and a church sat on the top with a tall spire that could be seen from the farm.

The wagon was driven into the courtyard of the large farm, and the children were helped down. The old grandmother took the children into the farmhouse kitchen and gave them each a glass of fresh milk, still warm and frothy from the cow. The farm labourers unloaded the furniture and other belongings and took the mattresses up to the bedroom. Julius' young cousin Ernst looked on with great interest as Stefan's piano was put in the living room where the old grandfather sat wrapped in blankets. After a good supper of home-smoked ham and home-baked bread the children were sent to bed.
'We get up early on the farm' said the old grandmother 'so you'll be expected to go to bed early here. You'll soon learn how we do things, and you'll each have your own jobs to do. Goodnight.'

Stefan and Julius were to share a room together. Julius' mother had already made up the beds with fresh linen on the mattresses that they had brought with them. She had brought up a jug of warm water for them to wash and showed them where the chamber pot was kept under the bed.

'The dog is let loose at night so don't try going across the yard to use the toilet; use the pot,' she warned.

Stefan's bed was by the window and he peered out into the yard where the labourers were still at work. He had only ever shared a bedroom with his parents and Peter before. He had never had a sleep over with friends. He missed his family but he thought it was going to be fun sharing with a friend.
'Will we have to go to school here?' he asked Julius sleepily.
'I don't think there is a high school in the village, but I think Mama said we'll be catching a train to town for school,' was the equally sleepy reply.
As they lay in their new surroundings they could hear the sound of the farm animals and the clatter of men working late in the yard.
'I hope I get used to all this noise,' said Julius grumpily 'or we'll never get any sleep. Close the window Stefan.'

Chapter Seven

The door burst open as Ernst launched himself into the room and jumped on top of Julius, still buried under his enormous feather duvet.
'Wake up cousin or you'll miss breakfast!' he shouted through the duvet.
'Get off you idiot!' groaned Julius. 'It's still dark, it can't be morning yet.'
'Well it is,' said Ernst sulkily 'and you'd better get your friend up or he'll miss breakfast too.'
Stefan had already woken from the noise and sat up sleepily.
'What's going on?' he asked 'is it an air raid? Where's the shelter?'
'It's not an air raid,' said Julius 'just my silly little cousin deciding to get us up stupidly early.'
'I'm not silly, and breakfast is on the table,' stated Ernst crossly 'so you can stay in bed and starve for all I care,' he added and went moodily out of the room.
'We'd better hurry,' said Julius, 'Grandmother has some strict rules and she can be pretty fierce.'
'Well, if the food is as good as yesterday, it'll be worth getting up at the crack of dawn for,' observed Stefan, who was already feeling hungry.
The boys hurriedly splashed cold water on their faces and rinsed their hands before getting dressed. They chatted while they

dressed and Stefan thought how different it was from home. The conversation there would have been about chores for the day, and what Peter would eat for breakfast. He loved his brother, but life had been very different before; when he had been an only child. Living here would be like having a brother his own age to play with all the time. He smiled to himself as he looked at Julius' slim figure and fine fair hair compared to his sturdy body and thick curly black hair; no one would mistake them for brothers.

'C'mon! I wonder what Grandmother will make us do to earn our breakfast today,' called Julius as he headed down the stairs.

The farm kitchen seemed to be full of people. Grandmother was standing by an enormous iron range, waving a wooden spoon, and shouting orders to anyone that came near her. Julius' mother had grown up on the farm and slipped easily into the role of a farm wife. She had obviously been up for a while preparing food for all the children. Anneliese was already sitting at the table next to Ernst. Several farm labourers were also at the table having breakfast. There were benches either side of the great table; Stefan and Julius squeezed on the end of one. Breakfast was definitely worth getting up for and the boys tucked in to home-cured ham, new-laid eggs, freshly-baked bread, cottage cheese and warm frothy milk.

'Eat plenty,' said Grandmother, 'we don't have time for lunch on the farm, so there won't be anything else till supper now.'

After breakfast Grandmother took the two boys outside and looked them over. She wasn't very tall but she was stout and strong. Her hair was plaited at the back, and then coiled into a bun at the nape of her neck. She stood with arms akimbo and pursed her lips in thought.

'You look strong enough,' she said to Stefan, 'when the prison labourers arrive from the camp, I'll get Pierre to show you how to mend tools. It's not possible to get anything new at the moment, because of the war; everything has to be mended. He's French but he's perfectly safe, in fact he's a very good farmer, so we've been lucky there.'

Stefan liked the sound of Pierre and he liked the idea of mending things – he was good at it.

Grandmother shook her head as she looked Julius over, clearly unable to decide what would be best for him to do. Finally she sighed and said 'I think you had best help your mother in the dairy, you have fine fingers; you should be good at milking.'

Julius was sent to the dairy to find his mother and Stefan was left in the courtyard to wait for Pierre to arrive. Surrounding the courtyard were a number of large barns. One had a kind of open porch section with all sorts of curious farm machinery underneath.

There was also a familiar ladder-wagon standing at one end. He was about to climb up on the wagon seat when he saw a tall lean man striding into the courtyard. He wore a thick military double-breasted coat over his shirt and trousers and had military boots. Stefan guessed that this would be Pierre. He had a pleasant face that lit up with a beaming smile when he saw Stefan. Stefan decided to introduce himself.

'Hello, I'm Stefan,' he announced 'If you're Pierre, then I've got to help you with mending things, Grandmother said so,' he added helpfully.

Pierre nodded and began unbuttoning his overcoat. Stefan suddenly wondered if Pierre understood German; he had never been any good at French. Pierre carefully folded his coat and placed it under cover in the ladder wagon. Then he rolled up his sleeves without saying a word. Just as Stefan was deciding that Pierre had not understood him, he beckoned to Stefan and said 'Come along then, I will show you how to use the axe.'

Stefan followed after him. 'I've used an axe before.' He said.

'Good,' was all the reply he got.

Stefan followed Pierre into one of the closed-in sections of a barn where many of the tools were stored, hanging in neat rows on nails in the walls. Pierre took down two axes. They had thick leather covers over the blades. 'First lesson, always muzzle your blade,' said Pierre warningly 'otherwise it might bite!'

With the head of the axe hanging down, Pierre held out the handle for Stefan to take. 'You must make sure the next person has a proper grip before you let go,' cautioned Pierre, demonstrating by not letting go of the axe until Stefan had gripped the handle firmly between two hands.

'Now carry it like this, in case you fall,' continued Pierre, showing Stefan how to grip the handle just below the edge of the axe head with the blade pointing away from him. Then he strode away in the direction of one of the fields with Stefan following, imitating his long loping stride.

Pierre stopped underneath a large old yew tree. There was a log store in the shade of the heavy green boughs, already well stocked with firewood. Pierre carried some wood out into the open.

'You need room to swing your axe,' he explained to Stefan, 'above your head and all around. The old woman bakes bread every week. She needs small pieces of wood for the oven. This can be your job. I will show you how to make them.'

After checking which hand Stefan used for writing, he showed him how to hold the axe with his right hand holding the handle just below the axe head and the left hand at the end of the handle.

'When you swing it,' explained Pierre 'your top hand will slide down to meet the other hand. Now look at a spot and keep your eyes on it — you don't need to swing hard.'

For the next hour Stefan and Pierre worked steadily and it wasn't long before Stefan was working nearly as quickly as Pierre.

By this time the sun had been up long enough to heat the ground and steam began to rise from the damp ground. Pierre looked up at the sky and grunted.

'Bath time for the cows,' he muttered. He nodded to Stefan to follow and strode back to where the tools were kept. Without speaking, he cleaned his axe head, indicated that Stefan should do the same, put the leather covers back on and hung them on the wall. Then with a slight jerk of his head he indicated that Stefan should follow him back out into the yard and into the cow shed.

Milking was over; there was no sign of Julius in the cow shed. Stefan wondered what he would be doing, and if he was having as much fun. Pierre led the cows out the back of the shed and down to the edge of the field where a small stream ran past the farm. Stefan was given a stick and told to keep the cows together at the back. There was a worn area on the bank of the stream where the cows gathered, and they all seemed to know where they were going, so there wasn't much for Stefan to do but follow. Once the cows were all standing in the stream drinking, Pierre handed Stefan a large scrubbing brush and showed him how to clean off the muck that had mainly collected around their legs and tail end. Several times Stefan managed to duck out of the way of a swishing tail, but eventually one caught him across the face. Stefan let out a cry of disgust and bent down so that he could wash his face in the clear water. At that moment the cows surged forward and nudged Stefan from behind. He tipped forward and fell headlong into the stream. He gasped as the cold water surged around him, and then felt himself being hauled up by his shorts as Pierre fished him out. He stood shivering on the bank while Pierre threw his head back and roared with laughter. Stefan laughed too, and from that moment they were good friends.

Pierre insisted that Stefan go and put on some dry clothes while he finished cleaning the cows and took them back to their shed. 'Meet me back under the tree,' he said 'we can have a rest.'

Stefan didn't take long to change, and got back to the tree before Pierre. He sat with his back to the tree looking out across the fields. The sky seemed bigger here than at home, there were no mountains or forests in sight, only acres of fields stretching into the distance. In one direction, there seemed to be a ridge of low-lying hills and he wondered if they were the border with France, the Siegfried Line that he had heard people speaking of. In the opposite direction, he could see the small village lying slightly below him, with the tall church spire rising above in the middle. Two working ponies were grazing in the meadow nearby. It was very quiet. It was as if the war was happening in another country and he wondered about his family.

Pierre arrived and sat next to him. He was carrying a small bundle wrapped in a piece of pudding cloth.

'The old woman said we could have some bread and ham, she knows that we don't get much for breakfast at the camp,' he said offering Stefan a slice of black rye bread and a thin slice of ham. Stefan took the bread, broke it in half and put half back.

'I had a good breakfast,' he said 'I am sure she meant for you to have most of it.'

Pierre nodded and sat back to enjoy the food, watching Stefan slowly chewing his piece of bread.

'I've never met a prisoner of war before,' observed Stefan, 'do you have a family in France?'

'Yes, and I believe I will see them again one day,' replied Pierre softly.

'What's the camp like? Are there many people there? How long have you been there?' asked Stefan, firing all his questions off at one go.

'Well I think it's an old military base, we sleep in rows in a long building. I don't know how many people are there – a few hundred I suppose. I have been there two years, six months, and twelve days – I've been counting,' answered Pierre. 'The old woman here gives me extra food when I ask - that makes it bearable, and I like farm work. Some prisoners have to work in the mines, I would have hated that. The only things I don't like are the May bugs at night.'

'May bugs?' queried Stefan.

'Yes, there seem to be a lot around here, they come in the window at night and bang around the room and crawl over your face if you let them,' said Pierre shuddering with evident distaste.

They continued working through the afternoon, Pierre teaching Stefan all the while. Then while Pierre continued with his work Stefan was sent back to the farmhouse and was able to spend some time with Julius until supper.

At supper, Pierre sat at the head of the table as if he were the head of the household. All the talk was about the jobs that needed doing and how to get hold of desperately needed materials for repairing machinery. After supper, Pierre put on his greatcoat and stuffed a package of extra rations from the old woman into his pocket and made ready to leave. As he opened the door to go he turned to Stefan saying

'You worked hard today, well done,' and then laughing, added 'and if you don't want the May bugs to bite, close the window Stefan.'

Chapter Eight

'Stefan! You're needed,' called the old grandmother from the kitchen. 'Come along, I need my expert egg collector,' she added jovially.

Stefan was only just awake and still pulling on his shorts when she called up. He quickly splashed some water on his face and used his wet hands to smooth down his hair before hurrying down stairs. He arrived in the kitchen out of breath.

'No need to break your neck,' laughed the old woman. 'Those devious hens have been hiding their eggs again and we need some for breakfast. Come with me and I'll show you where to look, they can't deceive me.'

The hay barn had open beams where the hay was piled up rather haphazardly, leaving odd spaces where the hens would go to lay their eggs.

'Look down there,' said the grandmother pointing to a gap of about half a meter high. 'It'll be dark in there, you'll have to wriggle in and then come out backwards. You're not claustrophobic are you?'

Stefan assured her that he wasn't and neither was he afraid of the dark. He crawled into the space, hands in front cautiously feeling for eggs. It was very dark and very hot. He moved very slowly, anxious not to break any eggs. His fingers felt a smooth round object and he carefully placed it in his left hand while feeling for more eggs with the right.

He could only manage to carry three safely and then wriggled backwards out of the hay tunnel on his elbows. The grandmother was very pleased and put the eggs in her basket. She seemed to have an uncanny knowledge of where the hens had laid their eggs and it wasn't long before they had collected enough eggs for a hearty breakfast for their expanding household.

There had been some new arrivals in the village, young women from Russia. They were billeted in homes in the village; they didn't have to stay in a camp like Pierre. The Russian woman allotted to their farm was called Marie. She had been given a room just across the landing from Stefan and Julius' room. Stefan had seen her arrive, and unaware that she was being watched, she had sat on the edge of the bed, covered her face with her hands, and wept with great soundless sobs. Embarrassed, Stefan had tiptoed quietly away.

Stefan proudly carried the basket of eggs into the crowded kitchen. He then squeezed onto the bench next to Marie. She was already tucking into some ham and freshly baked bread. She wasn't very tall, and at thirteen now, Stefan was almost the same height. But she was stockily built, with strong hands. Her fiery red hair, that seemed to shoot in all directions from her head, gave her a fierce look belied by the laughter in her eyes. She shuffled along the bench to make room for Stefan and smiled at him.

'I'm glad to see you know how to make yourself useful,' she said, nodding in the direction of the basket of eggs. 'You and Julius will be helping me in the drying barn today.'

'Well you'll soon have to manage without our help, we're at school next week,' said Julius, 'Mama has found a high school in Bad Bergzabern where we can go – it's just a short train ride,' he added.

'School!' exclaimed Stefan with evident horror, and to the amusement of everyone else in the kitchen. 'I hoped we could just go on working on the farm. I don't mind a bit of maths, but what's the point of history or Latin, and why do we learn English?' he groaned.

'I can help you with your English,' offered Marie. 'A good education is always important, whatever else is happening in the world,' she continued sagely. 'But in the meantime you will be helping me with the tobacco.'

Among other things, the farm grew tobacco. The leaves were put on long needles and strung up to dry in the barn. When it was ready, the leaves were carefully laid in wooden boxes, and the boxes were stored in a special room. After breakfast, the two boys followed Marie into the barn and they all set to work without talking. Stefan was the first to break the silence.

'Where do you come from?' he asked Marie.
'My family is from a small village in the Ukraine,' she said 'but my brother and I were taken away from our family and sent to have a good education because we were cleverer than the other children in our village. We didn't even see our family in the summer holidays because we were sent on pioneer camps, to learn how to work on farms like this one.'
'Is that how you learned English and German?' asked Stefan.
'Yes, and French, maths, science, engineering, music,' she answered, and then added pointedly 'and history.'
'Well I don't know how you even learned to speak in Russian,' chimed in Julius laughing.
Marie chatted about her old village for a while and Stefan could hear the sadness in her voice. Then she changed the subject, talking about some of the other Russian women in the village who seemed to have elected her to be spokeswoman for them because her German was good. Suddenly, Julius let out an exclamation.
'What's that?' he asked pointing to a pile of tobacco leaves that appeared to be alive, moving along the top of the table by themselves. As they looked closely they saw a nose, whiskers, and two black beady eyes peering back at them. Then a thick pink tail appeared, like a long worm out of the shadows.
'Rats!' said Julius with disgust 'I hate rats.'

Stefan hadn't moved; rats didn't bother him. At least, as long as they weren't in his bedroom they didn't bother him.

Marie took charge. 'Julius, put those boxes in the store and then go and get two broomsticks,' she ordered and Julius obeyed.

Then Marie and Stefan lifted up all the unhung leaves, shook them and put them up onto a high shelf. The exposed rats scurried into the storeroom where they were trapped. When Julius came back, Marie took one of the brooms and handed Stefan the other. Then she shut herself and Stefan in the storeroom.

'Can you kill rats?' asked Marie. Stefan nodded and they set about their gruesome work. Marie seemed to know that Julius couldn't have done it, and later, Stefan wondered how he had been able to, it was a horrible job.

When it was all over Marie sent him to his room to clean up and change. Julius had gone with Anneliese to collect windfalls in the orchard and the house seemed eerily quiet. Stefan scrubbed his hands, splashed water on his face and changed his shirt but didn't bother changing his shorts. It had been hard work and blisters were starting to show on his palms. He went to the open window and breathed in the fresh air. The air always seemed fresher here than at home, and not just because there were fewer air raids. As he stood there, he heard the sound of a cart pulling into the yard. He couldn't see what it was from their bedroom window, but he could hear that it was the cause of quite a commotion and he wanted to get a better view. He crossed the landing and went into Marie's room so that he could look out of her window.

In the courtyard, he could see that a young man had arrived by horse and cart, probably from the station. He was in military uniform and the Grandmother and Julius' mother were hugging and greeting him. Stefan guessed that it was Julius' uncle home on leave. He turned to go back into his room and glanced down at the bed as he did so. The piece of paper lying there caught his eye because the writing was in English. Wondering if his English was still good enough, he picked up the piece of paper and tried reading it. It seemed to be a list of map coordinates together with locations of Lorries and military installations. A wave of panic washed over Stefan as he realised that Marie had been collecting information; she must be a spy. His hand trembling, he placed the piece of paper back on the bed, trying to remember exactly where it had been and how it had looked. He went out of the room and pulled the door almost shut, hoping that no one else would go in, and hoping that Marie wouldn't notice that it had been opened. He would say nothing. He waited a few minutes for the shaking to stop and then slowly went downstairs.

Later that evening, after a noisy supper when everyone had been introduced to Julius' uncle, Stefan and Julius sat down to a game of chess. It was difficult for Stefan to concentrate, especially when Marie began showing the uncle how to dismantle his rifle so that he could clean it. How could she possibly know all these things? But Stefan liked her and he was determined to say nothing. When the two boys were safely tucked up for the night, Stefan asked Julius what he thought of Marie.
'She's a bit fierce looking, but I like her,' came the drowsy reply. 'And she's promised to help us with our English and Maths homework when school starts, so I hope she stays... and grandmother likes her... and mama... and me...' and he fell asleep.

Stefan didn't need to keep his secret to himself for too long. A few days later, his father arrived for a short visit. Stefan was coming in from the field, where he had been chopping wood with Pierre, when he saw him stepping out of the farmhouse kitchen door. Stefan was carrying his axe back to the tool shed to be cleaned and stored, but he let out an excited yell when he saw him.
'Papa! Over here! I can't run – I have the axe,' he called out.
'Be careful,' his father called back and went to meet him. Stefan put the axe carefully on the ground and gave his father a very warm

hand shake – he was too old for hugs these days.
'I'll come with you while you clean your tools,' said his father, and together they went into the tool shed.
'I know what to do Papa, Pierre – he's French – has shown me how to clean and sharpen the blade before I muzzle it and hang it up,' explained Stefan.
'Muzzle it?' queried his father.
'So that it doesn't bite,' laughed Stefan. He worked quickly while his father watched with interest, noting how much he had grown in a short time, sparking a feeling of anxiety. He was aware that the age for conscription into the army was getting younger, and there had been heavy set backs on the Eastern front where new conscripts were being sent. But he kept these thoughts to himself.
Stefan chatted as they strolled back to the farmhouse for supper, asking lots of questions about home, about Mama and Peter. They were both well and planning to visit before winter set in. A space at the table was found for Papa and he squeezed onto the bench next to Stefan. Pierre and Marie were both sitting down for supper, and so no one talked about how the war was going, although they knew that Stefan's Papa would have inside information. Pierre hardly spoke. Marie however, was comfortable speaking with him, keeping the conversation to music for which they both shared a passion.

'Stefan tells me you are good at chess,' said Papa after supper, 'would you care for a game?'
'A challenge, excellent,' said Marie enthusiastically and began setting out the pieces.
'Be careful Papa, she's very clever,' warned Stefan. Marie laughed, a deep rich laugh 'he knows me does that one,' she said nodding at Stefan. Stefan wondered for a moment if she had guessed what he knew, but there was only laughter in her eyes. Marie won the game with ease.
'I'm no match for a talent like yours,' said Papa, 'I'll stick to playing against Stefan. Come now Stefan, it's getting late, show me where your bedroom is and I'll say goodnight.' They went slowly upstairs together. Stefan was listening out for Julius; he desperately wanted to speak to his Papa alone. He wanted to tell him about Marie. He would know what to do. Stefan shut the bedroom door and sat down on the edge of the bed.
'Papa,' he began, 'I know something about Marie. I found evidence that she's a spy — and she should be shot. But I don't want to tell because I like her. She has promised to help us with our homework, and she helps the grandmother, and the grandmother likes her as well and...' his voice trailed away as his father hushed him and then spoke in an undertone.
'Firstly, don't speak of this to anyone else. I will decide what is best to do, and I like

her as well, so it will be best if we keep it to ourselves. Now, tell me quickly all you know. But before you do, close the window Stefan.'

Chapter Nine

To get to school, the boys had to catch a train to the nearby town of Bad Bergzabern. By train, it was just a short journey. But sometimes, following an air raid, they had to walk home. The school was in a building that had been converted in the early 1900s from an old palace. It was a magnificent building in the oldest part of town, with a tree-lined avenue along one side and a wide roadway in front. The palace was built around a central courtyard and there were stone archways through which you had to go to get into the courtyard. The archways were decorated with elaborate carvings. It had belonged to the family of the local Duke for hundreds of years and had old cellars that made ideal air raid shelters for the children. They took their exams in the cellars where the ceiling rolled over them in great stone arches. The light was dim and that suited Stefan. It meant that Mr Zwick, the maths and Latin teacher didn't notice when Stefan rolled up his sleeve to reveal the answers written on his arm. Stefan was fine with his maths - his music had helped him with fractions and Mr Zwick explained equations by writing them out as sentences - but he just couldn't remember the Latin verbs.

One morning, as Stefan and Julius were going through the ancient arch into the great courtyard of the old palace, Mr Zwick was just arriving on his bicycle with his two daughters. As he passed close to the stone sentry carved into the arch, the large floppy hat, that he always wore, caught on the stone and flew into the air. It looked just as if the stone sentry had taken a dislike to the hat and deliberately knocked it off. Stefan and Julius burst out laughing as Mr Zwick wobbled to an undignified stop. Stefan went to pick up the hat for his teacher. Preziosa, one of Mr Zwick's daughters, had jumped off her bicycle at the same time that Stefan had reached out for the hat. They collided, banging their heads sharply together.

After a stunned moment, Preziosa began to cry. Stefan felt his head; it was bruising already and would probably leave a bump.

'Come along,' urged Mr Zwick, 'we'll get a cold cloth on your heads upstairs'.

Stefan followed Mr Zwick and his daughter up a set of stairs that he had never been allowed to climb before. They went into a large circular room with tall elegant windows almost all the way round the walls. Stefan guessed it was one of the rooms in one of the great round towers that stood at each corner of the palace, with roofs that looked like enormous church bells stuck on top. There was not much furniture in it now, but Mr Zwick had a cupboard next to an old desk that was full of useful odds and ends. He took out some old cloths and soaked them from a jug of water that stood on the desk. The cloths were folded and the two children were commanded to hold their compress against their bumps. They both felt a bit silly. Stefan rolled his eyes at Preziosa to show what he thought of the compress and she began to giggle. Mr Zwick, observing that they must be feeling better, sent them back downstairs just as the air raid sirens began to sound.

From deep in the cellars, the air raids were only a distant rumble. Mr Zwick took the opportunity to give the children a maths test, hoping to distract their interest from the intensifying activity near the border with France.
'Where did he take you?' asked Julius as Stefan sat down next to him, still holding the wet cloth against his head.
'Into the round tower,' replied Stefan 'but we didn't go up into the bell,' he added disappointedly 'so we still don't know what's up there. But I did see where the steps are that must lead up into it.'
'It's probably just full of stuffy old books or paintings that the family didn't want,' observed Julius.
'Listen, after an air raid they nearly always send us home early. I bet we could get up there without anyone noticing if we were quick. How about it? We might not get another chance,' suggested Stefan conspiratorially.
'I don't know; I don't want to get into trouble and upset Mama' said Julius hesitantly.

'Oh come on, I don't suppose anyone will really care, and the building might be bombed to smithereens soon,' urged Stefan.
An hour or so later, Stefan and Julius hurried up the stairs where Mr Zwick had taken Stefan earlier that morning. There was a small door off the landing that Stefan had guessed would lead to the stairway up into the bell-shaped upper room. He was right; there was a spiral stairway leading straight up. Cautiously, the boys went up, not knowing if they would meet anyone else on their way. At the top of the stairs there was another door. Stefan slowly pushed it open, held his breath and peered into the room. What he saw was a large open space with absolutely nothing in it. Disappointedly, he walked into the room and looked about.
'There's nothing here,' he said, stating the obvious.
'Well what were you expecting, treasure?' asked Julius sarcastically, 'I'd like to go up that ladder and walk around on that gallery up there,' he went on, pointing up into the roof where a long gallery had been constructed all around the inside.
'I bet there is a good view from those windows,' observed Stefan, 'c'mon then, I'll race you up.'
Julius surprised Stefan by reaching the ladder first and climbing very nimbly up. Stefan followed close on his heels. The only light in the large room came from four windows that seemed to have been set to face each point

of a compass. Standing on tiptoe and wiping away decades of dust and grime, they peered through the old, distorted panes of glass. There wasn't really much to see other than roof tops of smaller buildings, but as Stefan leant on one of the window sills he noticed a small piece of metal lying under the dust. Curiously, he picked it up and blew the dust off to reveal an old coin.
'Hey, look at this,' he called to Julius, rubbing it clean on his shorts.
'Is it treasure?' asked Julius with genuine interest.
'Well it looks old, but I can't quite read what it says - I think that says Carl Theodor.'
'Look for a date,' suggested Julius.
Stefan spat on the coin and polished it with his shirt.
'I think it says 1777, that's really old.'
'Do you think it's worth anything?' asked Julius.
'No idea,' said Stefan, 'but Carl Theodor was important to Mannheim, I know he built the palace, my piano teacher told me something about him being important to the orchestra – anyway, it's so old, it's bound to be valuable.'
'So we did find treasure...' Julius broke off to listen. Someone was mounting the stairs. Stefan hurriedly put the coin in his pocket and put on his most innocent-looking face, ready to smile sweetly at whoever appeared. The sound of footsteps stopped, there was a

pause and then the footsteps seemed to move away again.

'Let's go while we can,' whispered Julius pushing Stefan back down the ladder in front of him. The two boys found their way back into the courtyard without speaking. There was no one about, all the others had long since left. The air raid meant that they had to walk home that day. They only spoke about the coin for a short while; there was no one they would be able to ask about it at the farm. Stefan decided to keep it somewhere safe and mention it to his Papa when he finally went home. He would tuck it under the lid of the piano, that way it would be sure to go home with them.

When they arrived back at the farm, there was a welcome surprise for Stefan. Mama and little Peter had come to visit. Peter seemed to have grown in just a few months. Mama had dressed him in a new outfit with lovely stripes. With the sun shining in his blonde hair, he looked to Stefan like a little angel.

"Shall I take Peter around the farm and show him the animals?" he asked Mama.

"If you can keep him clean," she replied with a warning tone.

Peter trotted happily round the farm, obediently holding Stefan's hand. They looked in at the cows and horses – but Stefan was careful not to get too close. They strolled up to the great yew tree to see the log store, and down near the stream – but not too close.

Later that afternoon, Stefan proudly presented Peter back to his mother in pristine condition.

Having returned Peter to his Mama, Stefan went into the kitchen for a drink of water. A few minutes later he came back outside, looking about him for Mama and Peter. Peter had wandered away to look at the beautiful pure white Polish cockerel that strutted proudly around the yard. Stefan watched his little brother looking with intense interest at the cockerel as it moved towards him. Then with horror, he saw the cockerel dive forward and peck him on the chin. Poor Peter howled with pain as Mama swept him up into her arms and ran into the farm house. The cockerel had pecked a hole in Peter's chin; blood ran down his clothes in red streaks and mingled with the stripes. Stefan couldn't believe that a cockerel could be so vicious. The old grandmother bustled about, patching Peter up very quickly and finding him something sweet to suck on to take his mind off the pain.
'Why else do you think people get cockerels to fight each other?' she asked 'they are worse than dogs – you should take a stick if you want to go close.'
Peter recovered from the shock, but the scar stayed with him for a long time. Mama and Peter stayed for a few days, keeping a wide berth of the cockerel, and then returned to be with Stefan's father.

Christmas came and went that year with very little excitement. There was no time on the farm for any holiday. No one in the village or at the farm put up a Christmas tree or any other decorations. At the farm, no presents were given and there was no special meal. The family went to church on Christmas Eve, but the church looked just the same as it usually did on Sundays; there were no decorations or a Christmas tree. The men sat on one side of the church and the ladies on the other side – everything was just as usual. Christmas at home had always been so special. There would be candles on the tree, Mama and Papa singing carols, accompanied by Papa on the guitar, and Stefan would play something on the piano. There were always gifts, no matter how small, and a special service in a decorated church. But this year it was very different, and Stefan missed his family more than he had in all the months before.

The boys continued to go to school when it was safe and the weather permitted. January was mild but dreary and a sense of dread seemed to hang in the air. Half-way through February, Stefan started to feel unwell. Everyone thought it was flu and he was sent to bed with plenty of hot drinks. But his glands swelled up and his tongue felt strange as if there was something on it. A few days after he had been sent to bed, Julius was sitting on the edge of his bed, telling him about what had been happening at school that day, when he suddenly stopped, leaned forward and pointed at Stefan's neck.

'Ugh! What's that? You've got red lumps all over your skin!' he exclaimed and leant forward to touch it.

'Go away,' moaned Stefan, 'leave me alone, I can't talk; my tongue's all swollen up and sore'.

'That's a rash' stated Julius 'I bet you've caught something nasty and then you'll have to miss loads of school, it's not fair.'

Later, it was Stefan that felt it wasn't fair. The doctor was summoned and confirmed what the grandmother had suspected; Stefan had scarlet fever. Poor Stefan was locked in the spare room and not allowed out so that he wouldn't infect anyone else. The only person he saw was Julius' mother who came with soft food that he could swallow and cool drinks to help lower his temperature. She washed him down, put lotion on his itchy skin and emptied the chamber pot. He saw no one else for a whole month.

'Why can't I see Julius?' complained Stefan on the first day.

'Because he might catch the fever as well,' replied Julius' Mama.

'Well then we could keep each other company' suggested Stefan hopefully.

'I'm sorry Stefan, but it might spread further, it is dangerous for me to come in here as it is,' came the disturbing answer.

'How dangerous is it?' asked Stefan in some trepidation, 'will I die?'

'Only people who are not strong die from scarlet fever,' was her reply and then in an attempt to reassure him, added 'you are a very strong boy Stefan, I have no doubt you will recover very soon.'

The skin came off his tongue leaving it sore and swollen. Then one day, to his horror and fascination, the skin began to peel off his hands and feet in sheets, just like layers of an onion. Stefan was quite happy to be missing school, although Julius did bring some Latin homework back for him, but there wasn't much to do all day.

As the weeks passed, with days spent in restless sleep, he watched the large cherry tree outside the window begin to bud. He watched as the buds opened and the tree bloomed with spectacular pink blossom and he knew that spring had arrived.

At the end of a month, the doctor came to check on Stefan's progress and gave him the all clear. Stefan was finally allowed out. The room was thoroughly disinfected. All the bed linen, and Stefan's pyjamas, had to be burned to get rid of any infection that might be lurking still. He was allowed to go down stairs and share meals with the others. The first evening, he went and stood by an open window, looking out at the yard watching that fearsome cockerel strutting around and wondering if his Mama had been told of his illness. Anneliese was sitting at the table ready for supper, shivering in the cool spring air.

'Brrr,' she said loudly, 'it's cold in here, close the window Stefan.'

Chapter Ten

Not long after Stefan's recovery, Papa arrived unexpectedly at the farm. Stefan was told that he would be returning to Mannheim with his father immediately. They were to travel by train and take Stefan's mattress with them.
'What about the piano?' asked Stefan, 'how will we get it to the station?'
'The piano will have to stay for now,' apologised Papa, 'we will have to try to bring it home another time... there isn't time now, hurry and pack your things.'
Stefan could sense his father's urgency and went to pack his suitcase without asking any further questions. It didn't take long; Stefan had very few clothes or belongings. Julius' mother helped him take the bed linen off his mattress and then his Papa carried it down stairs. Stefan took a moment to look around the room that had been home for the last year and tried to memorise all the details; he knew he wouldn't be coming back.

Then it was time to say goodbye. There wasn't time to take a last look around the farm, only time to say hurried goodbyes to Pierre, Marie, the Grandmother, Julius' mother, Anneliese and of course Julius. Stefan's mattress was loaded onto a small cart with his suitcase. A pony was hitched to the cart and Marie offered to lead the pony to the station and back. She seemed to sense Stefan's father's urgency and walked quickly ahead. They walked in silence, each with their own thoughts. Once at the station, Marie helped unload the mattress and turned to Stefan. Her eyes were wet and held a haunting look of longing.

'I miss my family too,' she whispered huskily, 'remember Stefan, when you are older, how you have worked pressing grapes alongside a Frenchman and a Russian, sworn enemies of your country. Work with them again and remember how you toiled together in peace.' Then without a backward glance, Marie led the horse and cart away back to the farm.

'Come', said Papa, 'we must be quick; this is the only train today.'

But the train was already full when it pulled in at the station. There were no seats and there was no room in the guard's van for the mattress.

'Help me with the mattress,' commanded Papa, speaking quickly 'if we put it on the couplings, we can ride on top, hurry.'

Between them they heaved the mattress up and over the coupling and buffers between two carriages and then climbed on top, hanging on to nearby pipes. The train moved slowly out of the station with Stefan and Papa perched on top of the mattress straddling the buffers.

As the countryside began to whiz by, Stefan found himself enjoying the excitement of travelling in this extraordinary way. His Mama would have been shocked if she had known.

The wind buffeted his face and blew his hair in all directions. The sound of the wheels on the track was so loud they could not hear each other speak.

After a while, the train began to slow and eventually came to a screeching stop at a small station at Winden. Stefan and Papa were able to give their arms a rest, and have a few minutes to relax. When the train started up again it seemed to be going the wrong way.

'What's happening Papa?' asked Stefan 'should we have changed on to another train?'

'It's alright, Stefan,' explained Papa, 'the train has to sort of double back and change lines here to go north.'

After a few minutes, they could tell that they were going a different way and not back the way they had come. The train picked up speed for a while and then slowed for the next station at Steinweiler. Nobody seemed to get on or off the train there and it was not long before the train pulled out of the station. By this time, some of the excitement had gone out of the journey for Stefan. He looked across at the fields flashing by. Babelroth already seemed to be a long way in his past and he was travelling at great speed into an unknown future.

Suddenly, Papa leant forward and grabbed his arm. He began pointing up into the sky. Stefan could just make out the unmistakable sight of a squadron of mosquito fighter planes that seemed to be following the train. The train began to slow.

'We haven't reached Rohrbach yet,' shouted Papa above the noise, 'get ready, we may need to get off the train'.

The train shuddered and screeched to a stop. Stefan could hear people shouting and doors opening.

'Quick, help me with the mattress,' ordered Papa, leaping down from the train as he spoke.

They dragged the mattress down from the buffers and then down the bank on which the railway ran. Stefan could see other people running into the fields to get away from the train.

Papa dragged their mattress towards a large chestnut tree and together they buried themselves behind it.

Stefan could hear the sound of the mosquitos as they flew over, strafing the abandoned train and the fields nearby. He heard a few cries, but mostly he could hear the drone of the fighter engines, the staccato explosion of cartridges, and the pounding of his own heart in his chest.

It didn't last long and there was a strange quiet when it was over. Silently, Papa and Stefan dragged the mattress back up the embankment to the train and heaved it back over the buffers. Without looking about them or at the other passengers, Papa helped Stefan back up onto the mattress and then climbed back on himself. Neither spoke; Stefan noticed that his hand was shaking as he reached out to hold onto the pipes again. He looked out at the field, now deserted, where the sun shone in golden patches on the grass and the wind blew a gentle breeze. The train slowly began to move, picking up speed but keeping slower than before. It seemed to Stefan to take much longer than the few minutes Papa had said it would be to reach Rohrbach. The train seemed to be at the station a long time. There seemed to be something important to unload, with a lot of shouting and people in military uniform running backwards and forwards along the platform.

Eventually the train set off once more, this time picking up a much faster pace. They didn't stop at Insheim, Landow or Knoringen, but as they were approaching Edesheim the train juddered and screeched to a halt again. Stefan could hear people shouting instructions to leave the train again.

'Leave the mattress,' shouted Papa, as he leaped down from the train, 'there is enough cover in the trees over there.' He was pointing to the edge of a small wood growing nearby. Between them and the wood was a field of maize that was almost fully grown. The plants were taller than Papa and Stefan and he wondered briefly how they would find their way through. But there was already a crowd of people heading the same way, trampling the crops in their haste. A woman with two young children was struggling to get down the embankment, slipping on the loose stones in her heeled shoes. Papa scooped up one of the children into his arms to carry and took the hand of the other child.

'Give the lady your hand,' he ordered Stefan 'hurry!'

Stefan took the lady's hand and helped her down the bank. She thanked him and then reached for her child.

'Stefan, put this one in my other arm,' he said without consulting the lady, 'we will be quicker if I carry them both,' he explained as he strode away with a swift glance up into the sky.

They all safely reached the cover of the trees before the drone of approaching aircraft could be heard. People huddled together in the shady wood and felt safe. A reconnaissance mosquito flew over a few times and seemed to use the train for a bit of target practice but nothing more. They clearly had another objective on this mission. When all was quiet the people boarded the train once more.

After Edesheim, the rest of their journey was uneventful and they eventually reached the main station at Mannheim, tired, dusty and very hungry.

Carrying the mattress between them, Stefan and Papa walked along the platform. Most of the old station had been destroyed by bombing. Outside, where the taxis used to queue, the road was eerily quiet. Stefan looked across at where the beautiful old baroque Mannheim palace had once stood. All that remained was a burned-out tangled mass of iron girders, heaps of stones, and remains of walls.

'We'll have to walk the rest of the way,' said Papa simply, 'but Mama should have a meal ready for us when we get home.'

With these encouraging words he led the way past the smoke-blackened façades of ruined buildings. Now and then a house had been spared, looking oddly out of place in the surrounding desolation. The streets were quiet. They met only a few people on their journey through the city centre. A slight smell of burning lingered and every gust of wind seemed to whirl up clouds of masonry dust.

Their route took them to a bridge over the River Neckar where Stefan had, before the war, often been swimming with his friends.

Stefan's thoughts turned to his friends. He had no idea if or when he would see Julius again. His friend Walter had been evacuated with the school to somewhere in the Black Forest where they were being given military training. Manfred had been evacuated to somewhere near Switzerland, but then had been sent to France to help service tanks on the front line. Stefan had heard that the boys sent to France had to sleep on concrete with just a bit of straw, even in the middle of winter, and some had been killed.

'Will I be going back to school?' he asked Papa.

'No, there is no school,' was the reply, 'I have found you a job in a factory that makes precision tools. You need to have a job to be able to get a ration card, and without a ration card there won't be enough food for you,' he continued.

Stefan was pleased that he wouldn't have to go back to school. He had enjoyed the work at the farm in Barbelroth, so he felt happy about the prospect of learning some new skills.

When they finally reached home, not much seemed to have changed. Their apartment block was still in one piece and the butcher still had his shop on the ground floor. Mama looked thinner and much smaller than he remembered, but he guessed that was because he had grown so much over the last year. His brother Peter had grown too, and become very talkative. Peter had been very excited that his big brother would be coming home and had lots of things to show him. Grandmother came to join them for their evening meal just as they were ready to sit down. Her wrinkled brown face, carved with laughter lines by a life-time of hard work and healthy living, smiled up at him.

'You've grown big and fat,' she observed, her dark eyes twinkling, 'they must have been feeding you well I'm glad to see.'

After supper, Peter was put to bed. Stefan stayed up to talk with Grandmother and his parents. They asked him lots of questions about his time at the farm, but very little was said about how life had been at home. Stefan realised that his childhood was finished. He wouldn't go back to school. His father had found him a job and he would soon have responsibilities just like his father.

Over Mannheim, air raid sirens began to wail. It seemed to have been a long time since he had heard them.

'More bombs!' spat Grandmother angrily 'Close the window Stefan.'

The drab wooden door in front of Stefan opened and he found himself looking up at a smartly dressed young woman who he had never seen before. Her hair had been plaited and fixed in an arch over her head in traditional style, but her dress was not traditional. She wore the military fashion worn by women in official positions although there was no sign of any badges of any kind of rank or position. She smiled at Stefan's papa, but hardly glanced at Stefan as he handed her a bunch of flowers that Papa had bought on the way. She took the flowers without looking at them and held the door open for Stefan and Papa to enter.
Inside, the strange lady led Stefan to a room at the back of the house. The room was clean and bare except for a bed and a chest of drawers.
'This is your room,' said the strange lady in a soft voice, 'and this is your bed.'
She opened the top draw of the chest and took out a pair of folded pyjamas and laid them on the bed.
'These are your pyjamas' she explained, laying them out as if she were ready to put them on him.
Stefan had never seen the woman, the house, the room, the bed or the pyjamas before and knew he would never see them again.

'You are very kind, thank you' he repeated according to Papa's instructions.

The strange lady gave him a brief nod, re-folded the pyjamas and put them away. As they went back through the hallway to the front door, Papa passed her a packet. She tucked the packet into her pocket without saying a word and opened the front door.

They exchanged polite goodbyes and walked away from the house.

'Do you remember the address?' asked Papa 'you must be able to tell anyone that asks without hesitation, as if you have lived there all your life.'

'Yes Papa. But does this mean I will have to go to school after all?' asked Stefan still feeling rather bewildered by the subterfuge.

'You need to live nearby to be able to register at the school in Weinheim' and Miss Schneider, who works in the office with me in Heidelberg, has agreed to give you a room in her house,' explained Papa patiently 'but that doesn't mean we expect you to live there or go to school in Weinheim, but it would be a good idea if you went to school just a few times in case anyone asks any questions.'

Papa had explained to Stefan that it was something to do with rationing cards and not wanting him sent to a military training camp as some of his friends had been.

'But will I still be working in Viernheim?' persisted Stefan.

'Yes, and being paid which will help at home,' replied Papa.

Stefan had found out that he had been brought home so suddenly because the English and American armies were in France, and the German army was retreating to the border that lay just a few miles from Barbelroth. He also knew that the Soviet army was closing in on the eastern front, moving towards Berlin. Some of the boys he went to school with aged just fourteen and fifteen were being sent into battle. Papa had found Stefan work in the hope that they could keep him from being sent away. His job was to help the maintenance man in a sack-making factory. It was dusty work, nothing like the work he had been able to do on the farm.

The air raids intensified over the winter. Stefan went a few times to the school in Weinheim and made friends with another Manfred who came from Lampetheim. On one of these days there was an air raid and the whole school had to go to a very large air raid shelter.

'Careful!' exclaimed Stefan, as Manfred nearly sat on top of him in the crush, 'I've got my New Year crackers in my pocket,' he explained.

'What on earth have you got those with you for?' asked an astonished Manfred.

'Well in case I need them,' answered Stefan vaguely 'they give off a good light; you

never know when you might need a good light.'
Stefan had told Manfred about his magnesium firecrackers but had not yet shown him any. Manfred was excited to see what they could do.
'Let's have a look then,' he pleaded 'when are you going to set them off?'
'They look best in the dark, so I was going to wait till later to show you,' said Stefan with a shrug of his shoulders.
'It's pretty dark in here,' pointed out Manfred. 'We could wait till after the all clear and then let one off after everyone has gone out,' supposed Stefan, 'I can't see the harm in that... I wonder if the crack will sound louder in here.'
Stefan began to set out the paper string and prepare the fuse. It seemed an age before the all clear sounded and people began to leave.
'Stand back,' commanded Stefan to Manfred as he lit the fuse.
The white light was spectacular, but the noise was deafening. Stefan and Manfred could hear terrified screams from people in the shelter who had not yet left.
'Now we're for it,' said Manfred 'quick, let's go before they start looking for us.'
The boys ran to the exit and then strolled nonchalantly out past the bewildered officials.

On a wet morning in March Papa came home with the news that Barbelroth had been occupied by American soldiers and that they were only days away from Mannheim. He was able to reassure Stefan that Julius and the family were safe and unharmed, but the farm and his piano had been badly damaged. Stefan wasn't worried about the piano but was relieved to hear that his friends were safe.

'What will happen to Pierre?' he asked Papa.

'I expect he will be sent home to France once they have all been checked,' replied Papa, 'but I don't know what will happen to Marie, it won't be safe for her to go back home. We have been ordered to defend Mannheim at all costs. You, Mama and Peter must leave here at once.'

'Stefan!' called Mama 'we are going to stay with my family on the farm in Wunschmichelbach. Come and pack your things quickly. There is no time to lose. We will have to walk. We can load up the old pram to take some things.'

Stefan hurriedly put some clothes into a suitcase, and then went to find his precious tools and other precious objects to put in the pram. He wasn't frightened, he found himself excited by the prospect of once again going to live on a farm. His time at Barbelroth had been one of the happiest times he could remember, and this time he wouldn't have to leave his Mama and Peter behind.

Papa wouldn't be going with them straight away but promised to join them as soon as

he could. He had his responsibilities to attend to.
Stefan was surprised at how quickly they managed to pack up so many of their things as they set off on the long walk. It was about ten miles to his grandmother's village and once they reached the forest the flat land began to change and they would have steep hills to climb. Out on the streets, Stefan was surprised to see hundreds of other families who were on the move, walking away from the city, carrying or pushing their precious belongings.

It wasn't long before they reached the familiar forest and Stefan found himself enjoying the adventure. Mama began singing some of her favourite folk songs to keep up their spirits and Stefan and Peter joined in. But for Peter, with his lame feet and still only five, it was hard work. Thankfully, Stefan was strong and fit; he perched Peter on top of their belongings and pushed his load with enthusiasm.
'Mama, do they know we are coming?' asked Stefan 'where will we sleep?' he wondered. He could barely remember visits when he was much younger and wondered if they would have room for the whole family to stay.
'No, they will have no idea what is happening, but I am sure they will help us, after all, they are family,' replied Mama 'we will have to help on the farm so that we are not a burden to them.'

'I know how to work on a farm,' stated Stefan proudly 'I'm sure we won't be a burden Mama.'

By midday they were getting tired and hungry. Mama had sensibly packed some food for the journey and they gratefully sat down for a picnic on the forest floor. She had also brought something to drink, which had made the load heavier for Stefan, but they all needed to be careful not to become dehydrated. The load was lighter after lunch, but Stefan could feel his arms and legs tiring. He gritted his teeth, determined not to let his Mama see how tired he was or let Peter become bored and fractious.
'What about a story?' he suggested to Mama. So Mama told a story about a young prince in a faraway castle who dreamed of slaying dragons, rescuing maidens and performing knightly deeds of heroism. As the afternoon wore on, Peter became drowsy. Stefan and Mama managed to rearrange the load in the pram so that Peter could lie down and sleep and for a while they continued in silence.
'I'll wait until you have settled in Stefan and then I feel I must go back to be with your father,' said Mama at length, 'we'll come back soon, but I am worried for him.'
'Shall Peter stay with me?' asked Stefan hopefully 'I am sure I can look after him.'
'No Stefan, he will be a burden to you with his lame feet, and I think they will be very

glad of your help on the farm now that many of the labourers will be leaving.'
They lapsed into silence, each thinking their own thoughts; each urging them self to keep going as daylight began to fade.

Colour had gone from the landscape when they finally reached the farm; the grey of dusk had washed it away. There were lights on in the windows of the farm house and voices could be heard in the yard. As they trod wearily through the farm gates, Mama began to weep softly from exhaustion and pent-up anxiety. A dog barked in the yard and a door was opened, spilling light out onto the cobble stones and Stefan's stout cousin Kate could be seen silhouetted in the door way.
As her eyes grew accustomed to the dark, she realised who it was.
'Mama!' she called back into the house 'it's Aunt Maria and my cousins; they are here in the yard.'
'Mannheim will fall, the Siegfried Line has been breached,' stated Mama 'please can we come in; we will work and not be a burden to you.'
'Yes, yes, come in,' said Kate taking Mama by the arm and almost lifting her in, 'and you' she shouted at Stefan.

The kitchen was not like the one Stefan remembered at Barbelroth. The table was smaller and had chairs rather than benches.

The room was long and thin rather than large and square and the iron range, at the far end of the room, was smaller. Stefan noticed that he could hear water running somewhere, but could see no taps in the sandstone sink, only a small spike from which water seemed to flow continually. But it was warm and dry and smelled of freshly baked bread. Mama collapsed gratefully into a chair and Kate thoughtfully arranged a pile of blankets and cushions in the corner for the sleeping Peter to lie on. Stefan allowed himself to relax and realised that the palms of his hands had rubbed raw from carrying his load – they were very sore.

After a light supper, Kate hurriedly made up some temporary beds on the kitchen floor – where it would be warm – and promised to sort out better arrangements the next day. She took a lantern and went into the yard to secure the farm for the night and check on the labourer's quarters in the next building. Then lights were turned off. Stefan found himself drifting off to sleep almost immediately. The last thing he heard was Kate speaking softly 'I'm so glad you're here. Goodnight, if you feel chilly close the window Stefan.'

Chapter Twelve

'Why doesn't someone turn the tap off?' Stefan thought to himself, 'we'll run out of water, we won't be able to put out the fires.'
Stefan had woken to the sound of continuously running water, and not immediately recognising his surroundings was confused and baffled by the sound. He opened his bleary eyes and looked around as he remembered their arrival at the farm the evening before. In the daylight he could see that it was clean and orderly but more poorly furnished than the farm in Barbelroth. His cousin Kate was washing her hands and face in the cold running water at the sink, evidently trying not to disturb the sleeping family.
'Good morning,' said Stefan politely.
'Good morning cousin,' replied Kate as she dried her face and hands. 'Wash your face and hands and you can help me get the breakfast, your Mama can rest for a while longer.'
She handed him a milking bucket. 'Do you know how to milk a cow?' she asked.
'I have worked on a farm before,' boasted Stefan.
'Good, but let the cows get used to your voice for a while before you start; they don't like strangers and will kick the bucket over if you're not careful,' cautioned Kate.
Stefan took the bucket and stepped out into the yard.

The cobbled yard was long and narrow. The cows seemed to be kept in the same long building where the family had been sleeping, but at the other end. On the other side of the yard was another building that looked like stables. Stefan wandered over and peered in. He could see horses and a few pigs. Next to this was a building that looked as if it was on stilts. It looked as if there were rooms above and below there was storage space where he could see bottles and food containers. He heard movement from above and looked up to see a young man coming lightly down the wooden steps towards him.
'Good morning,' said Stefan politely.
The young man looked up in surprise, he clearly hadn't noticed Stefan.
'Good morning, and who are you?' he asked.
'My name is Stefan. Kate is my cousin and we have come to stay for a while,' replied Stefan.
'My name is Jan and I'm from Poland. Have you been sent to collect milk?' asked the young man pointing at the bucket. 'I'll come and help, the cows don't like strangers,' he continued leading the way across the yard.
'Do you live on the farm?' asked Stefan, remembering Pierre who had to go back to the camp at night.
'Yes, up there,' he said pointing to the upper rooms of the building on stilts. 'I share with a Russian family — they have a baby — I expect you'll hear it crying soon.'

Jan led Stefan to a long stone trough with running water from a well. They both washed their hands and then went in to where the cows were. There were only five cows but it took a long time to milk them. Jan was quite right, they didn't like strangers. In the end Jan did the milking while Stefan talked to the cows so they could start to get used to his voice.

'There is only Kate and her mother here,' said Jan 'I'm sure they will be glad of your help. The Russians don't help any more, they just come for food.'

They had bread and ham for breakfast and Mama offered to help with the chores, but Peter still needed a lot of attention. Stefan could see that Mama was uncomfortable about staying.

After breakfast, Jan offered to teach Stefan how to fish. There was a small stream that ran through the middle of the village and by the side of the farm. It ran along the bottom of a deep ditch and through a tunnel under the road. On the other side the ground was flatter where it ran across the land belonging to a wealthy business man from Mannheim who owned a weekend house in the village. According to Jan, he and his wife led a secretive life and were rarely seen. Jan led Stefan to this part of the stream and waded in.

'Put your feet like this,' he said planting one foot either side of the narrow stream. 'The fish hide under the stones; make your hands into a shovel like this,' he explained demonstrating how he put his large long-fingered hands together, spreading his fingers apart, 'then just scoop the fish and stones up and toss them onto the bank.' Jan caught a few small fish. 'That'll do for my lunch,' he said pleased with himself, 'now it's your turn.'

Stefan waded in and planted his feet in the same place that Jan had stood. He bent over and copied the way Jan had held his hands.

'How do I know when there is a fish there?' he called up 'I can't see anything'.

'You just have to wait till you see a little movement, watch the stones,' called back Jan.

Stefan tried to guess where there was a fish and scooped up a pile of stones and hurled them onto the bank, soaking Jan at the same time.

'You need to be quicker than that,' encouraged Jan, 'and we don't need the stones, just the fish,' he added laughing.

After five fruitless minutes Stefan's back began to ache. 'I think I'll come back another day, you've already caught all the fish,' he said disappointedly. Stefan had a feeling that he wasn't going to be any good at fishing, but he liked Jan and was glad he was there.

A few days later, Mama and Peter returned home. Kate made up a bed for Stefan in the roof where the sausages were hung up to dry and other stores were kept. The toilet was outside at the back of the building and Stefan had to wash outside in the yard. As it was spring, the ploughing needed to be done. Kate couldn't manage all the jobs on her own and asked Stefan to take over the ploughing. She arranged for Edwin, an elderly man whose job was to police the land, to show him what to do. The farm had two horses and two oxen. The oxen were called Hans and Otto, Stefan liked Otto the best; he was small and round with a friendly face. Edwin showed Stefan how to harness the horses and oxen to the plough.

'It's not like ploughing on flat ground,' he told Stefan, 'the ground is all hilly here and you always have to plough uphill so the soil doesn't go down.' He showed Stefan how to start at the bottom and drive the horses up, then across, then up the other side.

'Stop!' he shouted on their first venture out 'do you see that big stone? You need to lift the plough over it or your plough will be torn apart. You have to be careful and keep your eyes open.'

It was hard work and although Stefan at fourteen was strong and sturdy, it took a long time and the animals could be unpredictable. Stefan had a good appetite, but the hard work made him extra hungry.

'Eat plenty Stefan,' urged Kate one evening after the ploughing had finished 'you need to rake over the ground next to get the dried up roots out.'

The door burst open and Jan appeared in the doorway, 'The Americans have taken Mannheim,' he announced with evident excitement, 'I'll be going home soon.'

Kate wasn't particularly interested; the war hadn't affected her too much. She had been forced to rely on foreign labour, but otherwise life hadn't really changed. But Stefan had mixed feelings. He knew it meant the war would soon be over, but he had no idea what was happening to his family.

'Well you haven't gone home yet,' observed Kate, 'so you can help Stefan with raking the field tomorrow; it's going to be very hot.'

As Kate had predicted, the next day was hot. Jan knew how to harness the harrow to the oxen and showed Stefan how it was done. The harrow had long spikes to rake the uneven ploughed fields; to smooth the soil and rake up dried roots. As they led the oxen out of the yard, steam began to rise from the cobbles in the heat. A fly buzzed in Stefan's face.

'I think all the flies have hatched out at once in the heat,' said Jan in disgust as he brushed flies away from his own face. Stefan became aware of a stinging sensation on his bare leg beneath his shorts and looked down. A large horse fly was drilling into his skin.

'Aargh I hate horse flies!' he shouted, slapping the fly from his leg.

'We'll be safe on the forest path on our way up,' said Jan 'the horse flies don't like the shade, but we'll be easy targets once we are on the field.'

'Poor Otto,' said Stefan, 'the flies are bothering him as well. Come on Hans, hurry up into the shade and we'll all be safe.'

They continued slowly up the forest path. It wasn't an easy path. It was steep and the rain had washed away much of the soil leaving large uneven stones that the harrow had to be lifted over to stop it breaking. When they turned off the path onto the field they found themselves back in the sunshine. It would have been a lovely day if it had not been for the flies.

'Go in front Stefan and lead Otto,' suggested Jan 'I'll follow behind and lift the harrow over the bigger stones.'

Stefan could see the flies starting to collect on Otto's face and he tried brushing them away.

'These flies are really pestering Otto,' he called to Jan, 'and Hans is getting fidgety as well.'

'They should be used to a few flies by now,' called back Jan as he lifted the harrow over a particularly large stone.

As they went backwards and forwards across the field, Stefan tried to keep the flies away, batting them away from himself as well. But there were so many that poor Otto's face was nearly covered by the time they had finished. They led the oxen back to the forest path that led straight back down to the farm yard. Stefan stayed at the front to guide the oxen, holding onto Otto's harness and Jan stayed at the back to take care of the harrow. The flies seemed to be swarming everywhere. Suddenly the oxen seemed to have had enough and began to charge down the hill.

'Look out!' called Jan 'get out of their way, they'll trample you or run over you with the harrow.'

But Stefan was being pushed along. The path was too narrow to get out of the way, one side went steeply up the hill side and the other fell steeply away. He was trapped in front. He knew that if he stumbled or tripped they would trample straight over him. His only hope was to hold onto Otto's harness and pull himself closer so that Otto could carry him down the path. They charged down, straight through the open gates and headed towards the trough. Stefan let go at the last minute as the two poor oxen buried their heads in the water to get rid of the flies. A moment later Jan ran into the yard and found Stefan climbing into the trough with the oxen, frantically splashing himself all over with the cool water. Jan stood and laughed at the spectacle for a moment before realising that the swarm of flies seemed to have followed them down the hillside and jumped in with Stefan.

Kate emerged from the kitchen and stood watching for a full minute before speaking.

'If that harrow is still in one piece, will you clean it and put it back Jan. Stefan, take Otto and Hans to the stable and then I have some more chores for you inside.'
Stefan pulled a face at Jan 'at least there won't be any flies inside,' he said laughing.
'Don't be so sure,' he replied 'you'd better take care to close the window Stefan.'

Chapter Thirteen

'Where did you learn to do that?' asked Jan as he watched Stefan cleaning and sharpening the scythe.

'Pierre taught me when I was at Barbelroth,' replied Stefan, 'he taught me lots of things.'

'I wonder if he has already gone home, I wish I knew when it will be safe for me to go home,' he said wistfully 'and wasn't there a Russian that you liked?'

'Yes, Marie, she's not a bit like the Russian family here,' said Stefan sadly. 'She helped me with my homework and knew all sorts of useful things; perhaps Papa will find out.' Stefan stood up and examined the edge of the blade 'that should do it; right fodder-cutting time. Are you coming?' he asked.

'I think I'll use my Sunday to visit Weinheim and see if I can get some news about what's happening out there,' said Jan optimistically.

Stefan set off for the field where the grass was left to grow as hay for the cows. If the weather was fine he quite enjoyed the early Sunday morning quiet and the rhythmic swish of the scythe. His other Sunday job was to clean the cows; there wasn't much straw so this was a less pleasant task for him.

That afternoon, since Jan had gone to town, Stefan asked to borrow Kate's bicycle to go and look for berries. The days had grown long and hot and dusty. Stefan felt guilty that he no longer thought about his family every day. Instead he was enjoying a free afternoon, winding his way up a gentle slope to where he knew he could pick a few berries and eat them by himself. He sat down on a patch of grass and enjoyed the quiet, there weren't even any flies to bother him; it was too dry. Then he thought he heard a fly, or a bee humming; it was too early in the year for wasps. The drone was getting louder and he realised it was man made. He had no idea whose side the planes would be on but didn't wait to find out. He jumped on the bicycle and started pedalling furiously back down the path. The path was long and straight and he let the bicycle go, enjoying the speed. Stefan could see a bend coming and the bicycle had started to wobble. He didn't want to break too sharply and skid, but the bicycle threw him off on the bend. He lay still in the dust for a while listening. The planes passed over. The bike was fine, but he had deep grazes on the backs of his hands and down his legs. He walked back home feeling sorry for himself.

Later that evening Jan returned from Weinheim with the news that the war was over. Kate and her mama wept with relief tinged with anxiety about the future. Stefan was shocked and not sure how to take the news. He wished he knew what was happening at home, or if he still had a home. A few days later, Mama and Peter came back to Wunschmichelbach to stay for a while. Mama didn't speak about home or Papa and Stefan decided not to ask any questions because he could see how upset she was; he was just glad to see her and know that she was safe. There was work to be done on the farm and Kate kept him busy.

'Get the cart out' ordered Kate, 'it's time to spread some of that lovely manure we've been collecting.'
Stefan obediently went to help. The manure pile at the back of the barn had been steadily growing and maturing into a soggy mass. It was very heavy to shovel up. The small cart was loaded up and harnessed to the horses. They had to make the familiar trip up the steep and narrow forest path to reach the field. Kate went to the front to lead the horses and Stefan stayed at the back to operate the hand break.
'Why do we have to put this stuff on?' asked Stefan wearily, 'what does it do?'
'It makes the soil warm which seems to make the ground softer for the seeds and helps put stuff back into the ground that the plants have taken out. But it's no good asking me how it works, I just know it does,' shrugged Kate.
'I suppose if I had stayed at school I might have learnt some biology, but they mostly seemed to want to teach Latin verbs or the history of kings and battles; I'd much rather

learn how to make and mend things,' observed Stefan. Later he thought how ironic it was that he had just said that when the cart hit a heavy rock and separated from the front part. Kate was still leading the horses.
'Kate!' yelled Stefan, 'the cart has broken.'
Kate halted the horses and looked back. The path was too narrow to turn in.
'I'll have to take the horses all the way up before I can turn them around,' called Kate. 'Can you get the cart back to the yard to mend it?'
Stefan had to tip the manure out before he could manoeuvre it back down to the yard; it would have been too heavy. He looked at where it was broken and saw that it needed a new place for the wooden pin that attached it to the harness on the horses. He went back up into the forest and found a small tree and used one of the horses to pull it down and haul it back to the farm. He enjoyed making the replacement part and drilling the holes. Kate was impressed.
'I didn't know you could mend things,' she said 'do you think you could mend the motor for the mill so we can grind the oats into flour?'
Stefan repaired the belt with shoelace and scraps of wire and managed to get the mill working again. This was exactly the kind of work he liked most.

One morning, not long after Mama and Peter had arrived back, a neighbour burst through the door just as they were all sitting down to a simple breakfast.

'It's the Americans! They are coming here – in tanks! You must find some white sheets, you must hang them out or you might be arrested, quickly,' she gasped, clearly out of breath from running. Then she turned on her heels and ran back, leaving the door wide open.

'Nonsense,' said Kate, 'I'm not hanging all my best linen out of the window - it's not ready for washing yet.'

'Please do it Kate,' asked Mama in a quiet voice, 'we can't risk any trouble.'

'Well it all seems like a lot of nonsense to me, I don't see why they want to bother with us, there aren't any soldiers here,' grumbled Kate.

'But Kate, it's not just soldiers they're looking for, it's anyone who was a government official or in any way involved with the party,' she explained and there was a great weariness in her voice.

'Well I don't hold with politics either,' said Kate sulkily 'I just look after the farm and Mama; I don't like all this nonsense.'

'Please Kate, I'll help you wash them later,' Mama offered.

'Very well,' agreed Kate reluctantly 'but I'm not happy about it,' she muttered as she went away to fetch her precious white sheets.

The sheets were duly hung from upstairs windows and Stefan went and stood by the road with the other curious villagers. Jan and the Russians were nowhere to be seen and Stefan felt instinctively that they were right to stay away. They stood silently and watched as two tanks came up the valley and slowly rolled by, heading up towards Oberflockenbach. Then just as silently people went home and shut their doors in uneasy anticipation of the unknown.

Just as she had promised, Mama helped Kate with washing her sheets, but Kate continued to mutter about it for days. Jan and the Russians seemed to have gone into hiding and since some of the stores had disappeared, Kate presumed that they had taken the food.
'Well I shall be glad to see the back of the Russians, that man was a nasty piece of work,' said Kate bitterly.
'I know a very nice Russian, she was very kind and helpful on the farm in Barbelroth' said Stefan.
'Well there is good and bad in every nation,' observed Kate philosophically, 'and I must admit that young Jan was a good worker and I shall miss him.'

A few days later, Stefan was helping Mama give Peter a bath in the washing copper. He was just pouring in some hot water from a pot that had been heating on the iron range when there was a sound of motor vehicles driving into the yard. Stefan stopped still to listen. He heard the sound of doors being slammed, unfamiliar orders being barked and the sound of military boots on the cobbles. The door was unceremoniously opened by a man in an American military uniform who swaggered in and gazed around the room with a languid air. He began speaking but although Stefan could tell it was English he didn't understand any of what was said. But their actions made it clear. They began looking in cupboards and drawers, turning things out onto the floor or the table. Poor Peter began to cry and Mama scooped him up in a towel and sat him on her knee in the furthest possible corner, trying to pacify him. The soldiers went upstairs and they heard Kate's protestations as cupboards and linen chests were turned out. The one who appeared in charge strolled over to Mama and said simply 'SS?' Mama shook her head and just kept saying 'no, no, there is no one here.'

When one of the soldiers who had been upstairs appeared at the foot of the stairs he held up Papa's camera as a trophy. Mama was furious. She carried Peter to Stefan and pushed him into his arms and then turned on the soldier, scolding him to give it back. The soldier was clearly startled by her response. The one in charge laughed and must have ordered it to be returned since it was handed back to her. Stefan handed Peter back to Mama and followed the soldiers outside.

'SS?' he asked. The soldier in charge nodded. Stefan indicated that he should follow him, he wanted to draw these soldiers away from

Mama who was clearly so upset. He knew the fat business man was never there so decided to let the soldiers believe that he might be someone to question. He led them across the road and pointed to the business man's weekend house. The soldiers broke into the house and began a search. They came out with a few trophies but the man and his wife were clearly not there – they hadn't been seen for some months and it was rumoured that they had gone into Switzerland. The soldiers left and Stefan went back into the farm kitchen. Mama was pale and trembling.

'It's alright Mama,' soothed Stefan, 'they've gone. I'm glad they gave Papa's camera back. Shall I heat up some more water?' he asked as he shut the door.

Kate could be heard complaining from upstairs as she tidied up the mess the soldiers had made. At the same time she was trying to reassure her own mama that the soldiers had gone and wouldn't be returning.

Stefan silently reheated the bath water for Peter and then carefully lowered him in. He found a bar of soap and tried to make Peter laugh by blowing bubbles. He went and found a cup for Peter to play with and a little wooden horse that could float on the water. He found a small flannel and gave Peter a bit of a scrub before lifting him back out to dry and wrapping him up in a large towel.

But it was Mama who shivered 'I'm cold,' she said simply 'close the window Stefan.'

Chapter Fourteen

Stefan listened to the cows contentedly munching the dew-soaked grass in the cool of the summer night. The cows preferred to eat at night when the grass was moist and the flies were dormant. The Americans had imposed an eight o'clock curfew, but that didn't worry him. The Americans never used their legs, they went everywhere with wheels and you could hear them coming. He took the cows up into the hills at night where it was dark and there were no roads suitable for American jeeps.

Stefan looked up at the moon; it was shining on the path nearby and he became aware of a large figure silhouetted against the moonlight. He froze, hardly daring to breathe while his mind tried to understand the image in front of him. It wasn't human, it wasn't a cow or horse or even a dog. Whatever it was it was bigger than Stefan. It moved its head slightly and Stefan caught a glimpse of a tusk. A wild boar! If it wanted to it could kill him in moments. He tried not to breath and waited. Then without making a sound it moved off the path and disappeared into the forest. Stefan heard nothing; it just seemed to vanish.

The next morning Stefan excitedly told Kate, Peter and Mama about his brief encounter with the boar.

'You just be careful,' said Kate, 'those beasts can kill a grown man if they're minded to.'

'Can I come with you next time?' asked Peter 'do you think he'll come back?'

'No you can't; you'll be asleep by then, and anyway if a wild boar came anywhere near you would probably be too scared to stand still and it would charge and we'd be killed,' said Stefan unfeelingly.

'No I wouldn't,' argued Peter.

'Mama, he should be in bed asleep when I take the cows out, shouldn't he?' said Stefan appealing to Mama.

There was no reply and as Stefan looked across at Mama he knew there was something wrong. She sat hunched in the corner of the kitchen looking wearily and distractedly out of the window. He wasn't certain but she seemed to be talking to herself as if trying to make up her mind about something. He finished his breakfast and told Peter to hurry up and finish his so that the dishes could be washed up and he could make a start on the day's chores. He then went and stood near Mama and waited for her to notice him.

'What is it Stefan? Does Peter need something, have I forgotten to do something?' she asked defensively.

'No Mama, but please can you tell me what's wrong. Is it Papa?' he said softly so that Kate wouldn't overhear.

'Oh Stefan,' groaned Mama, 'a few weeks ago while Papa was on his bicycle in the forest looking for mushrooms or berries to eat, some men came to the house looking for him. I don't know if they were American or Russian. They asked about his work but I couldn't tell them anything. I was so glad he wasn't home. But a few days later American soldiers came and arrested him.'

Stefan felt a knot tightening in the pit of his stomach as he had a sudden sense of intense fear. 'Why? What for?' he demanded.

'One of our neighbours has denounced him as a war criminal, but it's not true,' replied Mama weakly.

'Of course it's not true,' agreed Stefan angrily. 'Why would anyone do such a thing?'

'When people are hungry and frightened they might say anything, and you know that some people were jealous of the support Papa gave to the nuns and the orphanage,' said Mama 'he gave them a lot of roof tiles and materials for repairing the windows,' she continued sadly.

Stefan felt a surge of anger swiftly rising in him. 'But Papa is a good man; it's not fair,' he hissed angrily under his breath.

Over the next few days, Mama seemed to get worse. She didn't have the energy to do anything; she couldn't make decisions and began to complain about aches and pains. Kate became concerned and asked the local doctor to visit. Mama was taken to hospital. 'A nervous breakdown,' explained the doctor.

Stefan tried not to think about Papa in prison; there had been terrible rumours. He tried not to think of Mama in hospital. He tried not to think about the future at all. Instead, he took Peter down to the stream and tried to catch fish the way Jan had showed him. They caught nothing but had fun splashing in the water. When they had dried out in the sun, he sat Peter on Otto and took the oxen up into the fields – there was still work to be done.

In one of the apple orchards nearby, there stood an enormous granite bowl, about two metres across. Forty or so years before some Italian stonemasons had been hired to chisel out a granite dish to be used for a fountain at the foot of the ornate water tower in Mannheim near the palace. But when it was finished, they found that it was impossible to move because of the weight. So there it stood, abandoned under an apple tree, filled with rain water and a few early windfalls bobbing on the top. Stefan and Peter took their sandals off. Stefan lifted Peter up onto the edge of the dish and together they paddled in the sun-warmed water.

'Kate calls it the soup dish,' said Stefan.

'Can we have a soup dish when we go home?' asked Peter innocently.

Stefan wondered if they would ever go home. He looked up at the slowly ripening apples. They would be easy to reach from here, but he had no idea if he would ever taste one.

Stefan had less time for Peter over the next few weeks. The hay needed to be harvested and stored for the winter. A few of the men from the village came to help Stefan, including Edwin. Edwin took charge, directing the others although it was only Stefan who hadn't done this before. The horses were harnessed to the hay cart and led to the field. The hay was stacked on top. Stefan, as the smallest, had to perch on top to keep the growing mound even as it was stacked higher and higher. Then the horses and cart were led into the barn while the labourers used ropes to keep the load from tipping over as they rounded the corners.

Once in the barn it was Stefan's job, as the smallest, to go to the top to pull the hay up and stack it in place. It was very dusty in the barn and it was thirsty work. Edwin opened a bottle of apple wine from the store and passed it up to Stefan.

'This will help with the dust,' he said with a grin.

Stefan took a long drink. He hadn't tried it before; it was different from the apple juice Kate usually gave him, but he liked it. It was very refreshing. The hay kept coming and Stefan's throat became dry again. He took another long drink from the bottle and wondered why his legs were a little unsteady.

'We'd better get some food inside you,' Edwin called up, 'time for a lunch break.'

The workers piled into the small kitchen and sat down to home-baked bread and sausage.

'Give the boy some milk Kate, or he won't last the afternoon,' ordered Edwin.

'Have you been giving him wine?' asked Kate crossly.

'He needs something to wash down the dust up there,' said Edwin with a twinkle in his eye.

Kate put a jug of milk and a glass in front of Stefan.

'You'd better drink all of that or you'll be no good to anyone,' she said huffily.

Stefan obediently drank the milk. 'Does the milk help with the dust?' he asked.

'No, it helps with the wine,' explained Edwin helpfully.

After lunch Stefan was sent back up the ladder into the hay loft. It was hot dry work and the apple wine was very refreshing. His legs still felt wobbly later when he came back down the ladder but the milk had worked and he was able to walk back to the kitchen without coming to any harm.

'The milk worked Kate,' announced Stefan as he came through the door with a distinct wobble.

'Just so long as all the hay is in,' said Kate with suppressed laughter, 'supper is on the table.'

Stefan stood on the edge of the soup dish and reached up for an apple. The apples would be ready in another six weeks but he wouldn't be eating any of them. Mama had come out of hospital and they would all be going back down to Mannheim. Life for Stefan was about to change once again. He jumped down from the soup dish and tried to commit it to memory, hoping he would remember how it looked on that hot August afternoon. He looked up the forest track where he had so often taken Otto and Hans and he'd seen the wild boar. He wondered for a moment how many people had actually seen a wild boar. Then he strolled back into the yard. He looked in on the horses, cows and pigs. The cows knew his voice now and never tried kicking the bucket over.

Mama and Peter were waiting for him outside the kitchen door. Kate was wrapping up some last-minute provisions for them to take – she knew that food was scarce in Mannheim. Their belongings had been piled back into the old pram. Kate said a brisk goodbye and they set off. The journey would be different from the one they made in the spring. They would walk to Weinheim and then catch a train into Mannheim. For Peter, this would still be a long walk and Stefan knew Mama was not as strong as before.

When they arrived in Weinheim it seemed to be full of American soldiers and military vehicles. It felt very crowded and noisy after the peace and quiet of Wunschmichelbach. They managed to find a space on the guard's van and squeezed on with others who were not able to get proper passenger tickets;

but it was better than walking the whole way.

'Grandmother has been sleeping on the sofa,' Mama said suddenly.

Stefan didn't ask why, he could easily guess.

'Have you heard from Julius' family?' he asked instead.

'The farm suffered a lot of artillery damage and your piano is no good any more, but they are all safe,' said Mama 'but they have been told that the Russian labourers, who were sent back to Russia were all shot as spies.'

Stefan had such a clear picture of Marie in his head that he could almost imagine the sound. He found he had tears streaming down his face and hurriedly wiped them away. But he held on to the thought that Julius, Anneliese and their family were safe.

As they walked towards the familiar streets, Stefan tried not to look about him at the devastation. Compared to the vibrant clean colours they had left behind, they seemed to be walking in a world of grey and dust. The streets were empty apart from a few people who scurried away into the shadows as if afraid of being seen. As their apartment came into view, Stefan's spirits rose. 'Home at last,' he thought to himself. But Mama kept walking straight past their building.

'Mama!' called Stefan, 'where are you going?'

'I'm sorry Stefan, we have been told to move out of our old apartment. They say there are not enough of us for such a large apartment,

we have moved to a building opposite the church.'
'But we all squeeze in one bedroom anyway and you said grandmother was on the sofa,' objected Stefan.
Their new home was in the roof space of an old building not far from the old apartment. There were only two small rectangular windows in the roof; moths were coming in through the open roof light attracted by the dim light.
'At last someone strong enough' said grandmother 'close the window Stefan.'

Chapter Fifteen

Someone seemed to be strangling Stefan and a heavy weight pressed against his mouth so that he couldn't breathe. He woke to find his own hand lying across his mouth and Peter's arm twisted around his neck. They had been forced to sleep on the same narrow mattress as there was little else in the attic room. Stefan untangled himself and got up. He had got used to early hours on the farm, but Peter wriggled and stayed asleep. Mama slept fretfully on a thin mattress laid alongside grandmother's sofa. Stefan wondered how they would manage in this room if... no, when Papa came home. He began to look around to see what they could use for cooking and washing. There were no taps visible so he found a bucket and went to search for somewhere to get clean water. He found an iron pump in the yard and was pleased to find that it worked. He filled his bucket with what looked like clean water and carried it back upstairs.
He found a small wood-burning stove at one end of the room and a battered old kettle. There was a small pile of wood and a few fire lighter sticks. There were even some matches so Stefan lit the fire and put the kettle on to boil – he wasn't going to trust that the water was clean. He then took out the loaf of bread that Kate had kindly sent with them. He found an old knife and a cracked plate and sat at the only table in

the room. He let the water boil for a minute before pouring it into a cup that he recognised from home. The hot water washed the bread down very well and Stefan was pleased with his efforts so far. Grandmother woke up next and he was able to offer her a cup of hot water.

'I'm sure your Mama brought some tea leaves with her in a tin. Have a look in that cupboard by the stove; it'll taste better than plain water,' said grandmother 'and if you fetched up enough water for a wash I'll do that now. You can put some of that hot water in to warm it up for me,' she added.

Stefan poured a mix of hot and cold water into a large china bowl that they could use for washing and then hunted for some towels.

'There is some bread here from Cousin Kate,' he said, 'I'll go and fetch some more water while you have your wash.'

As he trod back up the stairs with the heavy bucket he wondered how easy it might be to plumb in a tap in the attic room. One of his uncles, Alfred, was a plumber; he would go and ask for advice as soon as he could.

Mama was awake when came back in and she smiled bravely at him.

'We need to go sparingly with the bread Kate gave us,' she said 'I don't know where we'll get money from to buy food, or even if there is any.'

'I can get a job Mama, I expect lots of places will be looking for strong labourers,' offered Stefan.
'Yes, you're right, and I'll look for work as a seamstress,' promised Mama.
'Do you think Uncle Alfred could give me work? I wanted to ask his advice about plumbing in a tap up here anyway,' asked Stefan.
'Yes, Uncle Alfred, he might. Do you remember the way to his house?'

A short while later Stefan set off in search of his uncle's house. It had been a few years since he had been there. It might not exist anymore; his uncle may have been killed. The concrete dust caught in his throat and he wished he had some of Kate's apple wine to wash it down. He was still only fifteen but he suddenly felt very old, as if everything were now his responsibility. He was surprised when he found his uncle alive and well; it felt like a small miracle in all the devastation around.
'I'm more than happy to take you on as an apprentice,' said Uncle Alfred, 'but I can't promise to give you any kind of pay. Mind you, some of my customers pay with food which you are welcome to share,' he offered.
Stefan was very pleased with the offer; he would be learning a trade and help to feed the family at the same time.
As he walked back to their new home, he glanced across the road to the church which

still stood on the corner of the square and he thought of Sister Karolina. He crossed the road and went into the church. The priest was there, lighting candles in the side chapel.
'Excuse me Father,' said Stefan politely 'do you know where Sister Karolina is?'
'I'm sorry my son, I don't know where she is and nor do I expect her back any time soon,' said the priest, 'can I give her a message when I do see her?'
'Will you just tell her that the orphanage roof has cost my Papa his freedom; he has been denounced as a war criminal and arrested,' said Stefan trying to control his voice but ending on a sob. He didn't wait for a reply but ran out and across the road gritting his teeth, determined not to show his emotions. He didn't blame the orphanage; he just wanted them to know.

Mama was pleased to hear that Uncle Alfred would take him on as an apprentice. Knowing that Stefan had a proper job seemed to give her renewed energy and she began to bustle about trying to make their accommodation habitable. Grandmother suggested that she take Peter into the forest, and if she could find a decent bag to carry them in, would come back with a fine selection of mushrooms for them to eat. Stefan set himself the task of making Mama a decent bed to sleep on. Grandmother had sensibly brought the axe with them and she showed Stefan where she had hidden it behind a cupboard. He found the old ladder wagon in the yard and set off for the forest with the axe carefully hidden. He walked along the road where his old apartment was and tried not to look up and then turned and walked down the old Post Road. As he walked past the cemetery he became lost in thought, remembering some of the fun times he'd had with Julius and Manfred. Suddenly he was pulled up short by someone shouting at him. The road to the forest was blocked and two American soldiers were guarding the way. Along the side of the road, stretching towards the forest were rows of American military vehicles and there appeared to be a whole camp setting up site at the far end of the cemetery.

As Stefan turned around he wondered if grandmother and Peter had found their way into the forest or had they been turned away as well. He couldn't understand how they could own the forest as well, shouldn't the forest belonged to everyone equally?

Instead of walking back up the Post Road, he turned right along Forest Road and then right again. It was a much longer route but it would be worth it if he could get into the forest without being stopped by American soldiers. He could see more military vehicles in the distance so he pulled the cart off the road and headed across an open field. He went across the field dragging the cart along the farm vehicle ruts, hoping that if they noticed him they would think he was a farmer. Eventually he was close enough to the forest edge to slip in. He knew almost straight away where he was, the forest was so familiar to him and he set off for a likely spot to find some useful wood.

Hours later Stefan emerged from the forest edge and began to cross the open field. In the distance he could see the small figure of his grandmother and a small boy limping by her side. He decided to cut straight across the field to get to his grandmother sooner and it wasn't long before he caught up with them.
'Grandmother!' he called out, 'wait!'
Poor Peter had been made to walk the long way round to the forest with grandmother. They hadn't been stopped at this entrance but grandmother was furious that the soldiers hadn't let them through on the Post Road.
'I've travelled along that road since I was a little girl,' she said crossly, 'I even remember the toll gate that we used to have to pass through.'
Stefan flattened out his pieces of roughly cut branches, put Peter on top and began to pull the cart along.
'But grandmother, did you find any mushrooms?' he asked.
'Yes,' she answered 'but I'm still cross,' she added with a laugh.

They got back to their new home just as the church bells rang for mass. They sounded much louder on this side of the square where they were closer to the bell tower.

'Will Mama be going to mass?' asked Stefan, 'she didn't go to church when we were in Wunschmichelbach.'

'You'll have to ask her, I won't be coming back down once I've gone all the way up those stairs; I'm cooking mushrooms and Peter can help me,' replied grandmother with asperity.

Stefan took the cart into the yard and unloaded the

branches he'd collected. He decided to try and split the logs so that he could use the flat side to support the mattress and have the rough part on the outside of the frame. He hoped Mama had brought Papa's tools with them and perhaps some nails as well. When he had split all the logs he pushed them into a corner and did his best to cover them up with some old sacking that he found. He planned to finish working on the bed frame the next day since Uncle Alfred wasn't expecting him for a few days yet.

The smell of frying mushrooms greeted him inside, reminding him of his old home.

'We can't live on mushrooms,' said Mama, 'tomorrow I will try to find work as a seamstress. Peter can stay with grandmother.'

All of a sudden Stefan wished they had his old piano. It would have been so nice to have played some of Mama's favourite tunes and listen to her sing. It had been a long time since he had heard her sing.

After their meagre supper, Stefan asked Mama if she would sing for them. She sang a lullaby for Peter and then stopped.

'What about Papa's guitar?' she said, 'I have it here. Do you think you can remember how to tune it?'

Stefan carefully took the guitar and tried to tune it. He didn't have a starting point so it ended up being a bit lower than it should but at least it was in tune with itself.

'Can you play it?' asked Peter 'I thought only Papa could play the guitar because you play the piano.'

'Papa showed me a few chords,' said Stefan hesitantly, 'but I don't know if I can remember them.'

Stefan put his fingers on the fret board the way he remembered and strummed. It sounded a bit out of tune but bearable.

'I think I can remember the chords for 'Little Hans',' he said and began strumming.

'I can't hear it,' said Peter sounding disappointed.

'That's because you have to sing with the guitar,' said Mama.

'Sing it, sing it please,' begged Peter.

Mama began to sing in her clear soprano voice and it seemed to fill the air. And then suddenly there seemed to be another voice singing with her. Mama stopped and listened. They all stopped and listened. A deep rich voice was singing out on the stairway and coming closer.

'Papa!' shrieked Stefan and Peter together as they raced to open the door. It was thrown wide and they both flung their arms around Papa's emaciated form.

Mama staggered forward hardly able to believe her eyes.

'How is this possible?' she asked.

'I'm not sure exactly, they just let me go. It was something to do with the church,' he said looking at Stefan.

Just then the church bells began to clang for the end of mass.

'The bells are very loud here,' said Papa, 'close the window Stefan.'

Lightning Source UK Ltd.
Milton Keynes UK
UKHW011846060721
386731UK00002B/82